SETTLEMENT-HOUSE NURSE

Donna Marker, R.N., was new to the settlement house and to its surrounding slums. She worked within the sheltering walls of the Pediatric Clinic, with infants and toddlers. Dr. Gar Breverman, the intense young psychologist in the counseling clinic, tried to open her eyes to the dangers of the teenage gangs with whom he worked. Fearing for her innocence, he made her promise not to get involved. Because she was deeply drawn to him, Donna promised . . . too easily. When a fifteen-year-old appealed for her help she could not stand aside. As a nurse, as a human being, she had to help. So she broke her hasty vow, never guessing that her compassionate instincts would trigger a chain reaction of violence that might cost her Gar's love—and her own life.

SETTLEMENT-HOUSE NURSE

Jane Converse

CURLEY LARGE PRINT
HAMPTON, NEW HAMPSHIRE

Library of Congress Cataloging-in-Publication Data

Converse, Jane.
  Settlement house nurse / Jane Converse.
    p. cm.
  ISBN 0–7927–1288–9.—
  ISBN 0–7927–1289–7 (pbk.)
  1. Large type books. I. Title.
[PS3553.O544S48 1992]   91–6326
813′.54—dc20   CIP

British Library Cataloguing in Publication Data available

This Large Print edition is published by Chivers Press, England, and by Curley Large Print, an imprint of Chivers North America, 1993.

Published by arrangement with Donald MacCampbell Inc.

U.K. Hardcover ISBN 0 7451 1775 9
U.K. Softcover ISBN 0 7451 1784 8
U.S. Hardcover ISBN 0 7927 1288 9
U.S. Softcover ISBN 0 7927 1289 7

Printed in Great Britain

SETTLEMENT-HOUSE NURSE

ONE

Donna Marker smiled as the last of the day's appointments, a frail Mrs. Rafferty with a gratifyingly healthy baby boy in her arms, started out the door.

A wave of balmy spring air flooded the drab office of the free pediatrics clinic. Through the open doorway, a beam of afternoon sunlight lent a sudden golden magic to the fading ecru walls and the worn, gray-brown wooden floor. There was no window in the small, high-ceilinged office-reception room; it was only when one of the young mothers of the Colton Street slum district came in or out of the room that the doctor and nurse on duty knew that winter had fled the sprawling gray city.

Mrs. Rafferty hesitated for a moment on the stoop, turning her pinched face back toward Donna. Timidly she said, "Isn't it *nice* out?"

"Beautiful," Donna agreed. It was the sort of day when even a dedicated nurse starts watching the clock an hour before closing time. "You'll want to get Ronnie outdoors every day now that it's warm and sunny."

The thin woman with the chubby infant in

1

her arms nodded. "Oh, I will!" She hesitated. "It's not easy, though. With no yard . . . and with all the other kids, I got so much work, when do I get time to carry him to the park?"

"Try," Donna said. "It'll be good for you, too."

Mrs. Rafferty nodded again, eager to let Donna know that she took medical orders seriously. Like so many of the other tenement women, she accepted advice with gratitude and with something akin to awe. If the medical people who were responsible for Ronnie's good health recommended walks in the park, she felt obligated to take them. Or, at least, to explain why the walks were impossible. "Anything Dr. Janis tells me . . . or if you say it . . . I . . . really do my best, Miss Marker."

"I'm sure you do. And Ronnie's proof of it. He's doing beautifully."

There was an exchange of polite good-byes, and then the door closed behind Mrs. Rafferty. Donna glanced at her watch. Six minutes past five. Gar Breverman was to meet her outside at five o'clock. Hastily, she replaced the Rafferty baby's chart in the file and snapped shut the appointment book on her desk.

"Proves my theory about spring."

Anxious about being late for her date,

Donna had almost forgotten about Dr. Janis. He had come in from the adjoining examination room quietly, his step as soft as his gentle, low-keyed voice. But, then, unobtrusiveness was his principal characteristic. With his sparse, almost colorless hair, his even, rather bland features, and quiet manner, Walter Janis not only appeared older than his thirty-odd years, but there was a tendency to be unaware of him as a physical presence. He and his work were so inextricably woven together that Donna thought of him only as "the doctor"; today, when the last patient had gone, she had seemingly taken along the doctor's reason for being, and, with this, his reality as an individual. Thus it was startling even to hear that modulated voice, and doubly amazing to hear a sentence that made no reference to their work at the clinic: "*Proves my theory about spring*" – whatever that might mean!

"I didn't know you had a theory about spring, Dr. Janis."

He moved closer to Donna's desk, the usually somber dark brown eyes lighting up to complement his smile. "Well, I do. I believe it should be reserved for cold and ugly places, where it's properly appreciated. That's not a theory, actually, it's a . . ." Dr. Janis twisted his face into a mock scholarly

3

scowl, pretending deep concentration. "A philosophy. If I had gone into politics, I'd have used it as a platform. I still may."

Enjoying the unexpected nonsense, Donna encouraged him. "Down with Spring in the Country! Save Spring for the Slums!" She laughed. "Be sure to get a campaign manager who doesn't lisp, for that last one."

"I'm quite serious. I spent part of my childhood on a Michigan farm. We had beautiful meadows, about ten acres of woods. It was beautiful with snow on the ground, beautiful with rain pelting the trees; winter, summer, fall . . . it was always beautiful."

"But more so in the spring, you will admit?"

"With the cherry trees in bloom? Oh yes. But we didn't really *need* spring, you see. We weren't starved for beauty. Then, while I was serving my residency, I lived in California, where the silly natives only *think* they appreciate spring. But how can they, when it's green the year round? A little gilt on the lily, that's all. A slight diversion for poets and peasants." The doctor crossed the room, opening the door and looking out into the street. "But, *here!* A few weeks ago the air was clammy cold and the sidewalks were all ridged with dirty, frozen slush. A barely articulate woman like Mrs. Rafferty opens this

4

door and says, 'Isn't it *nice* out?' Triter than Tennyson, but felt clear down to the soles of her shoes. And she probably hasn't seen a tree yet, mind you. Can you imagine the magic that's taking place over in the park?"

"Dr. Breverman would have an answer for that," Donna said.

"Yes. He'd say the muggings are more spirited at this time of the year. The hoodlums smile while they're stomping you." Dr. Janis shook his head dolefully and closed the door, returning to the desk. Donna had risen and was slipping a lightweight coat over her uniform. "Gar Breverman's exceedingly cynical, as psychologists go."

"I don't imagine he's exposed to much sweetness and light, working next door," Donna pointed out. "He's probably had to develop a tough shell."

Walter Janis nodded, but his expression was dubious. "Working for the city, getting all the rough cases the psychiatrists reject. I expect you're right. We're fortunate . . . giving shots to babies instead of being shot at by disturbed kid gangsters. He's had a few close calls, you know. One paranoiac youngster . . . boy about fourteen . . . pulled a knife on him just a week ago. Fortunately, Breverman got his Ph.D in psych but he's studied karate also."

5

"I hadn't heard," Donna said.

Dr. Janis looked almost hopeful. "Oh? I thought you ... spent quite a few of your evenings together."

Donna smiled, feeling color rushing to her face. "We've had dinner together three times and seen two movies."

"Just ... casual dates?" It was Dr. Janis's turn to look uncomfortable. "Oh, look, I don't mean to sound like I'm prying." Then, with a short, embarrassed laugh, he added, "But, of course, I am."

"Just casual dates," Donna said. At least, to the young psychologist they had been nothing more; she didn't add that meeting Gar Breverman had been the highlight of her two months at the McKittrick County Welfare Clinic.

Dr. Janis appeared suddenly shy again. So ill at ease, in fact, that Donna found it hard to believe the rumors about him: that he had been engaged to a socially prominent debutante, had built up, in two short years, a lucrative pediatric practice in the city's most fashionable area, and had even enjoyed a brief reputation as a man-about-town. The grapevine at the clinic indicated that the doctor's engagement had exploded during a jealous fit on his young fiancée's part. The girl's resentment had

6

been leveled at a competing "mistress" who still held Walter Janis in her clutches: his profession. Apparently freed of the necessity to collect fat fees, the pediatrician had looked around for needier babies in larger quantities – income secondary. The clinic was made to order for a doctor who placed service above salary. Ironically, the regulated hours made it entirely suitable for a married man whose wife resented sharing the evening hours with patients. And now Dr. Janis seemed destined for bachelorhood.

He sounded a far cry from his short-lived playboy role now, as he asked, "Ah ... you wouldn't be ... going out with Dr. Breverman *this* evening?"

"He's supposed to meet me outside," Donna said. She made the statement sound almost like an apology.

"Oh. Oh, well. Fine. That's just fine. Wonderful weather ... good for a drive along the river." Dr. Janis busied himself by opening a filing cabinet and flicking the manila folders importantly. "You really should have him call for you here inside the office."

"Oh, Dr. Janis! Now you sound like *he* does."

"It's a ... rough neighborhood, Miss Marker."

7

"It's still daylight out."

"I know, but you want to be careful. You drive to work, don't you?"

"Yes. I didn't today, though."

"Oh yes. Because of your date tonight. I hope you took a cab in the morning."

"On a beautiful April morning? In a neighborhood that appreciates spring? I walked. My apartment's just on the other side of Colton Park. Faces the park, actually."

"The park's the dividing line," Dr. Janis said absently. He didn't have to explain that Colton Street, west of the five-acre square of playgrounds, trees, and small lagoons, was considered respectable, if not fashionable. East of the park sprawled the old brick buildings that enclosed the McKittrick County Settlement House and Clinics: the gymnasium and craft centers for young people, the Youth Employment Bureau, a social hall where senior citizens gathered to play checkers or, twice a week, to watch old travel movies, the psychological-counseling office presided over by Gar Breverman (working in co-operation with city juvenile officers), and the pediatrics clinic.

Catty-corner from this drab, cement-surrounded complex rose the equally hideous brick structure that housed the

County Hospital. Donna had received her training in this toughest of all schools; the ex-classmate with whom Donna now shared her apartment, Pam Hollis, still worked there as a surgical nurse on the eleven P.M. to seven A.M. emergency shift.

Following Colton Street farther to the east, amid the rumble of trucks on their way to the nearby produce and industrial districts, one came to the twenty-odd square blocks that were the shame of the city, and also its sorrow. Here the ramshackle wooden porches of dilapidated tenement buildings rose layer upon layer, criss-crossed with wash lines of grimy blue work shirts and limp diapers. Perhaps the lines of hung-out laundry were a blessing, shielding citizens form both ends of the street. After dark it was no-man's-land, vainly patrolled by the totally inadequate police force, the stamping ground of the worst elements East Colton Street had produced. And if the park was no-man's-land, it was certainly no woman's. (Discounting, of course, the local girl gang known as the Tabby Cats.)

"I'm going to be here another hour," Dr. Janis offered, suddenly losing interest in the files. "If you'd rather wait inside. . . ."

His uneasiness increased Donna's anxiety to leave. "Thank you, Doctor, but I'm late

9

now. I'm sure Dr. Breverman's outside by this time."

He agreed. He was the doctor again; quiet, colorless, impersonal. Walter Janis exchanged polite good nights with his nurse, and Donna hurried out into the caressingly warm air, convinced that her superior's "theory" was sound; spring was painfully needed in this narrow, blind side street that bordered the side of the building. Across the street, the newspaper-littered parking area reserved for settlement-house personnel had a crying need for April's touch also; and a half-block in the opposite direction, where noisy trucks stirred the grime of East Colton, a sense of rebirth was so desperately hungered for that, glimpsing its ugliness, the generously endowed farmers of Michigan might have been moved to relinquish their rights to the beautiful season.

Gar Breverman was nowhere to be seen. Donna walked the few yards from the well-baby clinic door to the psychological-counseling-unit entrance. She thought of waiting for Gar in the reception room outside his office, but changed her mind when she reached the door. He had probably been delayed by a patient; he might resent her intrusion. It occurred to Donna that since *she* was late, Gar might have walked across the

10

street; he might be waiting for her in his car.

Her guess proved to be wrong, and Donna had started back across the street when she saw the gang. Not all of them; according to Alice Oleson, the Girls' Activities Director at the settlement house, there were at least fifteen girls identified with the Tabby Cats. At the moment, only four were present, but among them was Tabby herself.

Easily recognizable by the "cat uniforms" – tight black turtleneck sweaters, even tighter elasticized black Capri pants, the vests of sleazy cloth-imitation leopard skin – the quartet had lined themselves alongside the clinic building. They were leaning against the brick wall in a variety of indolent poses, apparently finding themselves with nothing better to do, although a doorway just around the corner would have led them to a whole world of active recreation. But from all indications, Tabby Lacer and her followers used the settlement house as a hangout; its facilities were sneered at as square.

Crossing the street, Donna realized that unless she made an obvious detour to avoid them she would be forced to crowd past the girls on the narrow strip of sidewalk bordering the building. But why avoid them? They were just kids, probably rejected kids, playing tough to cover up their adolescent

11

confusions. Donna lifted her head, smiled directly at the group, and continued her course.

Embarrassingly, there was no response to Donna's smile. The girl known as Tabby lifted a cigarette to her mouth and dragged at it with slow deliberation; there was no glimmer of warmth or recognition in her eyes – arresting hazel eyes with a slight yellow cast that would have given her a feline appearance even if she had not underscored them with heavy black upsweeping pencil lines. Her hair, dyed a cheap straw yellow, then back-combed and lacquered into an incongruously flashy balloon style, weighed heavily over a slender face that looked as though it had never been exposed to sunlight. She wore a luminous white lipstick, giving her full mouth a freakish appearance and emphasizing the already prominent eyes. Tall, voluptuously built, Tabby's figure dominated the scene physically, and evidently her reactions were dutifully emulated by the members of her gang.

There was no smile on the face of the girl who had been pointed out to Donna as "Nicki." A sullen red-head, whose green eyes lay under a heavy application of blue-black mascara, and whose coiffure was a slightly modified imitation of Tabby's, Nicki viewed

12

the world with a cold, reptilian expression. She seemed to look beyond Donna, as though this stranger were beneath her contempt.

A short, plump brunette with a rather blank, though not unpleasant, face was the third member of the group. The fourth, also a brunette, seemed strangely out of place. Perhaps it was her imagination, but it seemed to Donna that the tiny, olive-skinned girl with long, loose-flowing brown hair had started to return her smile. Then, as if she had realized that a show of warmth would have cut her off from the others, the pretty youngster lowered her eyes quickly, obviously uncomfortable.

She could have taken lessons in discomfort from Donna at the moment. As she approached the group, Donna heard a low-keyed whistling sound from Tabby. It became an extended, rhythmic whistle, which was joined by the other girls. It took a few seconds for Donna to realize that the tune was one to which she'd heard neighborhood children chanting, "The worms crawl in, the worms crawl out. . . ." The insolent beat was timed to her footsteps. She was being watched and ridiculed, the whistling chorus intended to make her nervous.

Ignoring the sound, making no attempt to change the rhythm of her walk, Donna reached the cement sidewalk and turned in the direction of the clinic doors. There would barely be room to squeeze past the girls, she saw. But stepping off the walk into the street would have implied fear on her part. Resolutely, she kept on going. The whistling stopped. She heard Tabby's deep, raspy voice:

"I'm sure sorry *I'm* not a nurse."

The red-haired girl, Nicki, took up the chorus. "Yeah. I bet she carries bedpans good." Her voice had a thin, nasal twang.

"Sure wish *I* looked like June Allyson." That was Tabby again, mocking. "How 'bout you, Jo-Jo? Could you make time witha cute doctors, uh? You had a cute shape like that?"

Her plump pal made a snorting noise. "I bet *she* does awright. I bet her and the doctor keep the door locked all day."

There were meaningful guffaws, followed by a series of obscene remarks. Donna struggled to keep her composure, almost feeling the girls' breath as she marched in front of them. None of the girls stepped back to make room for her, forcing Donna to balance herself precariously on the curb as she walked. She was almost past them, eager to escape the humiliating taunts, yet forcing herself to move unhurriedly. She heard Tabby snicker, "I bet all the patients flip over nursie-wursie. They prob'ly *fall* fer her! Like *this!*"

14

It happened too fast for Donna to know whether she had lost her footing or had been tripped. As the word "fall" registered in her mind, she felt herself tumbling forward. In the next instant, she was sprawled next to the curb, her handbag exploding its contents as it flew to the pavement. There was raucous laughter from her audience.

Miraculously unhurt, Donna pushed herself up to a sitting position. She was too stunned to be angry. She felt too dazed to respond to the derisive comments from behind her back:

"My, my! Ain't that a *shame!*"

"Nursie faw down."

"Didn't watchum her footsie-wootsies."

Slowly Donna got to her feet, bending over to gather up her compact, lipstick, and billfold. As she reached for her key ring, another hand swooped before her, picked up the keys, and started to hand them to her.

"Drop it, Julian!"

The throaty order had come from Tabby. Donna turned to see that the command had been issued to the pretty little Cat with the long brown hair. It was quite obvious that the girl had felt ashamed of the tripping incident and had jumped forward to help Donna.

"I said *drop* it, Julian!" As the order was repeated, this time menacingly, Donna saw the younger girl (she couldn't have been

15

more than sixteen) hesitate for a breathless second. There was bewilderment in the girl's eyes, but there was fear, too. The delicate fingers opened up to release Donna's key ring and the keys jangled once more to the concrete. Donna retrieved them, dropping them into her bag and pretending not to notice that Julian's tawny complexion had turned a deep scarlet.

Several yards away, a door opened.

Tabby's next directive was muttered from between her teeth. "Let's be missing."

There was a split second during which the quartet in black was present, and in the next breath Donna knew that they were gone. In the brief interval between, she heard the determined pounding of Gar Breverman's feet on the cement and his booming voice demanding, "What the devil are you doing way out here? Don't you have a brain in your silly head?"

She was standing up now, attempting to look undisturbed, with Gar towering above her, asking questions in a tone half critical and half concerned.

"Couldn't you have waited next to your office? Inside *mine?* I'm sorry I'm late, but . . . ye gods, girl, you don't go strolling around here with that hyena pack on the loose! Did they rough you up? What happened?"

"*Nothing* happened," Donna assured him.

Gar ran a hand through a mop of curling black hair, a mannerism he indulged in whenever he was faced with a puzzle and determined to solve it. Pinned under the scrutiny of those all-knowing blue eyes, it was difficult to pretend nonchalance.

"Level with me, Donna. What happened?"

Donna sighed. "All right, I'll tell you later. Could you drop me off at my place for a few minutes? I'd like to change."

"You look fine to me," Gar said, taking her elbow and helping her across the street toward his car.

"I'm still in uniform. Under the coat."

"Oh. Oh, sure." Gar paused, stopping to look Donna over critically. "You also have a hole in your stocking," he said after a while.

Donna glanced down to see that she had torn one of her nylons at the knee. "I . . . tripped and fell," she explained weakly. "Stupid accident."

"Uh-huh. I'll have to hear all about *that*, too."

Gar steered her toward the parking lot, Donna knowing in advance that at least part of their evening would be devoted to an increasingly familiar argument.

TWO

"What I keep trying to get across to you," Gar said while they dawdled over their after-dinner coffee, "what I don't think you clearly understand, is that the East Colton Street district isn't a kindergarten playground. It's a jungle. To a lot of characters in the neighborhood, staying on your feet simply means kicking the other guy down before he kicks you. And you *don't* wander around thinking you're going to change all that with a friendly smile or a pat on the back."

"I wasn't trying to change anything tonight," Donna insisted.

"I'm relieved to hear that." Gar's sarcasm could sometimes cut the air like a cleaver. "From now on, I'll meet you inside your office. Okay?"

"Gar . . . that's not going to help."

"It'll save you a lot of unpleasant moments." Gar lifted a corner of his mouth in a lopsided grin. "To put it mildly."

"But that isn't solving any problems. It's not *helping* anyone. It's just running away from a . . . from a responsibility."

"Donna?"

18

"Hm?"

"Listen. You don't have to tell me that the girls you tussled with tonight need help. They do. You don't have to tell me their families have given them a kick in the face, or that society has rejected them. In a lot of cases it's all too true. Not in all cases, but in a good percentage. I'll buy that. But I've worked with kids like Tabby Lacer . . . treated their families. You know?"

"I don't get your point."

"I'm telling you that you can't tackle them head on. We have social workers, experts in juvenile delinquency problems, sociologists, therapists . . . teams of experienced people knocking themselves out over the problems these kids pose. And sometimes, with all of our accumulated knowledge, in spite of all our coordinated efforts, we find ourselves beating our heads against a stone wall."

"I don't see what that has to do with me. With my . . . interest in these kids."

"I'm sure you don't. You're absolutely convinced that it hasn't *occurred* to the rest of us . . . those of us whose careers revolve around juvenile gangs . . . that we've never even *thought* of your approach. Treat them like intelligent, normal human beings. Show them they *aren't* rejected. Offer them friendship and affection."

19

"You ... *do* believe in that approach?" Donna was appalled by the very suggestion that he didn't.

"Not in a dark alley, honey. Not with a switchblade pressed against my midsection." Gar smiled ruefully. Almost patronizingly, it seemed to Donna. "Sometimes it takes years of patient work before you can crack those hard shells ... before you can even *talk* to some of those kids. Some ... face it, Donna ... some you can't get to at all."

"I won't buy that."

"I didn't think you would. Amateur psychologists, do-gooders, fanatical missionaries, and softhearted nurses. All alike." Gar released his breath wearily. "You have to learn the hard way. While you're learning, let me point out that some of the girl gangs we've dealt with make the male hoods look like eagle scouts by comparison. I mean ... *really* vicious. Sadistic. What you experienced tonight was a mild, mild sample. Or don't you ever read the papers?"

Donna set her coffee cup into its saucer resolutely. "I think those girls tonight were all bluff."

Gar pressed the heel of his hand against his forehead and closed his eyes for a moment, feigning resignation. *"Mama mia!"*

"If I could talk to them individually ...

20

when they're not trying to impress each other with their toughness ... I could make them see that they're wasting their lives. I'd ... convince them that I'm their friend first. Prove I can be trusted. Then I'd ..."

"Donna?" Gar sighed once more, behaving as though the subject was so deep and complicated that he didn't know where to begin explaining its complexities to one of the uninitiated. "Donna, it's not that simple. Believe me. Not with a tough cookie like the Lacer girl. You smile at Tabby, she thinks you're weak. She's got to keep trampling the weak. That's her only reservoir of strength. Show her a kindness and she wonders, 'What's *your* angle?' In her book, everyone has an angle. Appeal to her conscience? You couldn't find it with a high-powered microscope."

"*Everyone* has a desire to be good ... to be accepted."

"In their own milieu," Gar pointed out. "In their own frame of reference. Tabby's good! In the eyes of her gang, she's *great*. She's done time."

"Time ...?"

"In a girl's reformatory. Most of her girls don't have records ... yet. That makes her a heroine."

"If she's been arrested, doesn't that prove

21

she isn't too bright? The other girls could be made to see that."

"To them she's a queen. Picked up for shoplifting, resisted arrest, assaulted a police matron. She's not quite eighteen, Donna, but she's a respected leader. Her boyfriend heads the Colton Street Conquests. *He's* done time for car theft. Where do these kids go from there? Upward and onward. Bigger crimes, bigger stakes, more glory and probably longer terms. Spitting harder into society's eye. That's how they won their current prestige, that's how they're going to gain more."

"They can be shown . . ."

Gar reached over the table to take one of Donna's hands into his own. "Sometimes they can, but don't you try showing them, girl. You're thinking in normal, loving, socially adjusted terms. You can't even begin to fathom the way their minds work – the results of their conditioning. Just . . . stay away from them. Okay?"

Donna shook her head. "No. Not if I can help . . . even if it's just *one* of them . . . help them get straightened out."

"You can get hurt, Donna."

"Not if they know I'm only out to help them."

"Ohh, brother . . . why do I waste my breath?" Gar moved his head from side to side

22

slowly. "You're too stubborn, too energetic, too enthusiastic, too naïve, too unqualified, too inexperienced, too . . ."

"You forgot 'too stupid,' " Donna reminded him curtly. She felt the customary annoyance rising within herself, the resentment that Gar invariably stirred with his protective warnings and his lofty professional arguments.

Still, he didn't let go of her hand, and Donna decided that their often-repeated argument was a waste of time. Since she had come to work at the clinic she had been fascinated by, and, for some incomprehensible reason, attracted to, the tough, cynical, offensive gang kids who used the settlement house as a hangout. She had listened avidly to Gar's stories about rumbles between rival gangs, about the peculiar loyalties existing among the members of each clan. Observing, curious, asking questions of adults who attempted to reach, reform, and rehabilitate these delinquents, Donna had become convinced that a sincere, warmhearted amateur like herself might have more success than professionals who had two strikes against them because the kids resented their authority.

But why was it necessary to rehash the subject with Gar? If an opportunity presented

23

itself, in spite of all Gar's fearful warnings and officious advice, she knew she would not be able to resist the challenge. Perhaps she had failed tonight. But there had been too many of them. One by one, privately, under the right circumstances, she was certain to win them over. That frightened little girl tonight . . . the one Tabby Lacer had called "Julian." Why, she had wanted to help pick up the scattered handbag things! Given some time with a girl like that . . .

Why even discuss these ideas with Gar? Why waste this precious time? She was in love with him, desperately hoping during her hours apart from him that he might grow to return her love. And here she sat, his hand pressing hers firmly, and she was bickering with him! Creating an unpleasant atmosphere because he apparently cared enough about her to be concerned with her safety!

Gar was grinning at her. "You're right. I forgot 'too stupid.' In this one area only, understand. I'd be just as unqualified if I had to . . . immunize a squalling baby against polio."

"Okay." Donna returned his smile. "Each to his own."

"You don't meddle with malcontents and I won't go around pinching babies with a hypodermic needle. Is that a deal?"

"It's a deal, "Donna promised.

They shook hands on it, and nothing more was said about Donna's desire for a one-woman reform campaign. They talked about Gar's work with families in need of psychological counseling, of the odd characters who wandered in and out of their respective offices, and even of Dr. Walter Janis and his abrupt turnabout from socialite's darling to tenement mothers' godsend.

With the top of Gar's black convertible lowered, they cruised along the river drive. To their left, a million lights twinkled, delineating the outlines of the city; long white necklaces of light marking the streets, squares of light rising in orderly rows to create a fairyland of skyscrapers. On their right, the river moved in dark laziness, only occasionally reflecting the blurred images of lighted warehouse buildings, steel barges, or a crossing bridge, heavy with traffic. Above them, the stars offered glittering competition to the city's lights. It was April, heady and warm, descended upon a metropolis that had lain chilled and rigid under the frozen mantle of winter. With the melting of the ice had come a reawakening of the senses and a stirring of emotions. Seated beside the handsome young psychologist, Donna made no protest when he pulled the car into a parklike promontory overlooking the river and turned off the motor.

In the dim light afforded by the dashboard, Donna noted Gar's sheepish expression.

"Do I look like a cat with canary blood on its whiskers?" he asked. He laughed, and his arm fell easily over her shoulders.

"More like a wolf," Donna corrected.

He feigned a deep growl. "You wouldn't believe me if I told you I'm strictly interested in the view?" Without giving Donna a chance to tell him she hoped he was interested in more, Gar pulled her close to him, folding her in his arms and planting a warm kiss on her lips. "I'm not terribly excited about the view," he said after a while. "Are you?"

Donna admitted that she was not, and he kissed her again, his own breath coming hard as her arms encircled his neck.

Disappointingly, Gar said nothing about being in love with her, not even suggesting that he preferred Donna's company to that of anyone else. But she had hungered too long for Gar's embrace (their other dates having ended with cheerful, impersonal good nights) to insist upon any formal declarations. It was good to be with him, exhilarating to feel the strength of his arms around her, flattering to luxuriate in the traditional expressions of love, even if love was not Gar's motivation.

She loved him too hopelessly now to demand more, lest she frighten him off.

Still, later, when she found herself alone in her room at the apartment (Pam Hollis being on duty at the hospital, there was no one to confide in) Donna wondered if her anxiety to please Gar Breverman had not been a mistake. Where did you draw the line between rejecting a man and thereby losing him, and letting him take your kisses for granted?

Eager, full of life, possessed of too much energy and too many ideas, she was her own worst enemy, Donna concluded. Even her desire for involvement with the mixed-up kids from East Colton Street demonstrated this characteristic, which might very well be her most serious weakness.

Yet she was forced to admit to herself that if Gar asked for another date, even though she knew perfectly well that it might end in a futureless session of what teen-agers called "making out," she would accept. Just as she would follow her instinct to help out the Tabby Cats and their ilk, if a chance came up. This, in spite of a solemn promise to the contrary – a promise she had made tonight to the man she loved.

THREE

Donna was crossing the parking lot the evening after her date with Gar, when she noticed the girl Tabby had referred to as "Julian" leaning against a parked car, next to Donna's Chevy sedan. At first sight of the black Tabby Cat uniform, Donna drew a quick breath. Then she noticed that the girl was alone, and that she looked both eager and ill at ease.

It was quite obvious that she was waiting for her, yet when Donna smiled and said, "Hi," the tiny brunette with the long, snarled hair pretended that she was looking across the lot, as though she were expecting someone else. She responded with a faint "H'lo," then started to walk away.

"You weren't waiting for me, were you?" Donna asked.

Startled, the girl's expression revealed that she had been doing exactly that, but she said, "Me? Oh no. No, I just . . . I was waiting for somebody else."

Donna unlocked her car door. "I see. Beautiful out, isn't it?"

The girl drew closer to the Chevy, still

28

hesitant. "Yeah . . . it sure is." The friendly, impersonal question seemed to bewilder her.

As Donna started to get into her sedan, the girl must have had a change of heart. "I was just gonna say . . ." She paused. The wide brown eyes resembled those of a frightened woodland animal.

"Yes?"

"I mean about yesterday. What happened."

"Oh?"

"I wanted to tell you . . . I mean, the way it was . . ." Suddenly the girl blurted out, "I'm really sorry. About your purse and all that."

"It wasn't your fault," Donna assured her. "You didn't trip me, and you tried to help me pick things up."

"Yeah. Well . . . I didn't wanna act chicken. . . ."

"Is that why you took your orders from Tabby?"

Embarrassed, the girl covered up with a show of resentment. "I don't take orders from nobody." Then, softening again, her confusion pitiful to watch, she amended, "See, when you wanna get along, you have to sometimes . . ."

"Do things that you don't like doing?" Donna asked coolly.

"Yeah, sort of. I mean, no sense gettin' the kids sore at you. See, you either join up or you don't join up, and . . ."

"Do you have to join up?"

The small face contorted as the girl's mind groped for an answer. She looked terribly thin; without makeup, she also looked pitifully young, so that the female hoodlum outfit she was wearing appeared ludicrous. After a long pause she said, "Boy, they make it rough for you if you're just . . . you know . . . all by yourself. I didn't really want to get in with Tabby and those kids. I mean, don't ever say I told you this. They're really okay, most of the time, but, like, some of the stuff they do, say like yesterday . . . I'm not *like* that."

"I'm sure you aren't," Donna said. Then, to end the girl's agony of groping for an explanation, she said, "My name's Donna Marker. What's yours?"

"Ann. Ann Julian."

"Were you going home? Can I give you a lift somewhere?"

Ann shook her head. "No . . . I don't live around here. I mean . . . we have a real nice house . . . pretty far from here." Lying amateurishly, she added a suddenly inspired location. "Over around Fairview Boulevard."

"You're a long way from home, then." Fairview Boulevard crossed one of the more affluent residential areas of the city, at least twelve miles to the west.

Blushing, Ann said, "Yeah, I am. I only hang around this neighborhood *sometimes*. I don't *live* around here."

If she had plainly stated that she lived in one of the ugly tenement flats around East Colton Street, and was desperately ashamed of the fact, the truth could not have been more apparent. Donna decided not to press the issue. "Well . . . if you want to ride to the bus line, or . . ."

"No, it's okay. I don't have to get home until seven. My mother goes to work at seven."

"Oh, she works nights?"

Again, Ann found it necessary to explain. "Yeah, she . . . she's a manager in this real classy dress shop. I have to stay with my kid brother. I mean, we have a maid, but" – Ann's speech deteriorated into a jumbled half-whisper, as though the lie was too weak to merit enunciating out loud – "it's better if I'm there, 'cause this maid . . . she isn't . . . too hot when it comes to kids."

Donna nodded her understanding. She was overwhelmed with curiosity about the girl . . . the child, actually, for Ann Julian's size and naïveté gave the impression that she was not even as grown up as the average sixteen-year-old. She was curious about Ann's home, her family, her schooling, her involvement with

31

the hardened girl gang. But the interview had already been difficult for Ann, and Donna decided not to risk frightening her off. Still, following her usual impulsive pattern, she said, "I live across the park. Someday when you aren't too busy, why don't you drop by?"

"*Your* place?"

Ann's stunned reaction brought a smile to Donna's face. "Why, sure. My roomie and I have a lot of records you might like to hear."

"Man, that would sure be neat. What would I do ... call you up first, or what? Like, I wouldn't wanna come around if you had a big date or ... you know, somebody really important was there."

"Here." Donna brought a note pad and pencil from her handbag and scribbled her phone number. "Call first and then you'll be sure."

Ann accepted the slip of paper as though someone had handed her the deed to a uranium mine. She stared at it for a moment, and Donna could have sworn her eyes had misted over. She read the number out loud, pronouncing each one carefully, apparently wanting to verify its correctness. Then she looked up at Donna with a beseeching expression that asked if this was really so; she had been invited to a nice place and this was the telephone number to call, and when she dialed *this* number it would not turn out to be a hoax, for she was genuinely wanted.

"That's right," Donna said. "Make it soon, Ann. Bring your little brother along if you like. My roomie's a fiend about baking cookies, but she's on a diet, so they pile up. We could use a small boy around the place."

That was laying it on a bit thick, Donna decided later, but extending the invitation to Ann's brother had somehow solidified the matter. Ann had repeated an awkward apology about "that crumby deal about your purse stuff," and had hurried off in a direction calculated to convince Donna that she did *not* live in the slum east of the settlement house.

Where Ann was headed, how she would spend the two hours before she was due home to "supervise the maid," and who her companions would be during the interim, was anybody's guess. Donna drove home with a satisfied, almost gloating feeling of having applied a technique far beyond the scope of the professional social workers at the settlement house. Gar would have been impressed; once she had genuinely befriended Ann Julian and steered her on a more constructive course, he would be immensely proud of her.

Meanwhile, if and when he asked her for another date, it would be wisest to say

33

nothing about the new project. Vaguely, Donna remembered something about a half-hearted promise not to meddle in an area where the results were usually unpredictable ... and sometimes, according to the smug professionals, dangerous.

FOUR

Ann Julian came to the apartment on the following Sunday afternoon, dutifully and dubiously phoning in advance.

She came alone, dressed in a threadbare, too-tight plaid skirt and a neatly pressed white blouse that had seen better days. Torn between awe and a need to impress Donna and Pam Hollis with the luxuries of her own home, she alternately admired the furnishings and announced that "we have almost the same thing at our house." She let herself be persuaded to stay for dinner, but was too nervous to eat any of the roast and trimmings her hostesses had prepared. At six o'clock she made an abrupt departure, making some flimsy reference to "meeting friends of mine." Donna closed the door behind Ann with a sinking sensation, half convinced that the teen-ager had been grossly uncomfortable during the visit and would not accept the invitation to come again.

Donna rejoined Pam, who was lingering over coffee in their small dinette. "Well. We tried." She sighed audibly. "I don't know that we accomplished much."

Pam shrugged her shoulders. "We said all the right things, didn't we?"

Donna's friend remained as unsmiling and unflustered during her free hours as during her daily tour of duty in Surgery. Thoughtful, and sometimes coldly analytical, she served as an excellent balance for Donna's spur-of-the-moment enthusiasms. With her ash blonde hair drawn into a neat, conservative coil, and her light blue eyes enhanced by pale, classic features, she was a study in pastels, and her personality was well suited to her subtle coloring. Pam had the well-scrubbed, scrupulously clean appearance one associates with surgical nurses, and her grave outlook was a matter of personal pride with her; if someone had told her that she lacked a sense of humor, she would have agreed in a soft, serious voice, without considering the remark in the least derogatory. To Pam, nursing was a serious business, life was a serious business; all decisions required deep, logical consideration. She approached everything with this placid, ultrasensible attitude. Yet she was not without compassion or interest. Her judgment of Ann Julian proved that:

"She was miserable, Donna. We bent over backwards to make that kid feel at home, but she still felt out of place."

Donna shook the coffeepot, decided that it contained enough for another cup, and poured it for herself. "It's too bad she got herself all wound up in that fantasy about her home life. She spent most of the time trying to cover up slips in her story."

"Pull up a chair, Reformer," Pam invited. "Admit Dr. Breverman was right."

Donna seated herself at the table. "I dunno, Pam. Maybe even the softest of these kids is unreachable."

"How can you help the girl if she's too ashamed of her – of the most basic things – her home, her family life? How do you know she was telling you the truth about *anything?* About school, for instance. She says she hasn't dropped out of school yet, but she may as well. Then we start encouraging her to at least get a high school diploma and off she goes . . . telling us that she's a top student at Fairview High. You *know* she doesn't go to Fairview, Donna. So how can you be sure she goes to school at all? And did you notice how she skirted all your questions about that . . .

36

gang she belongs to?"

"She's ashamed of that, too," Donna pointed out. "At least that's a hopeful sign, isn't it?"

"Then why is she a part of it?" Pam demanded.

"She might be . . . afraid to quit."

"If it's that bad, she should go to the police."

"I don't mean physically afraid, Pam. I mean . . . it's the center of her social universe right now. Heaven knows what her home life is like. In the gang she's accepted . . . she belongs. Until she finds a better replacement . . ."

"You offered her one, didn't you?"

"Oh no! No, in her eyes we're a couple of old fuddy-duddies . . . more like her schoolteachers than friends her own age."

"Well, I think you ought to forget it, Donna. You can't do anything for that girl. She didn't think enough of you as a friend to be honest with you. From where I sit, you wasted your day off and you didn't accomplish Thing Number One. I offered to cut her hair and set it – remember? You tried to give her that darling green suit of yours. How could she accept?"

"I know," Donna admitted. "With the story she'd cooked up, she couldn't take any help from us. At least she has pride."

"Dishonest pride. Ann doesn't *want* your help."

"Maybe she got herself into a position where she can't take it. But she must be reaching for something better in life. Why else would she have come here?" Mulling the situation over in her mind, Donna added, "You're right about not being able to do anything for her as long as she keeps up the false front. And I s'pose she'd really despise me if I found out for myself where and how she lives."

"Don't even think about it," Pam warned. "I've had a little experience along those lines, old girl." The graceful features were suddenly marred by hard, embittered lines. "I don't have to go into detail."

Donna shook her head. "No. I guess not."

They seldom discussed the young med student with whom practical, sensible Pam Hollis had fallen so insanely in love during her first year as a graduate nurse that most of her salary, over and above the most necessary expenses, had gone toward his support. Sympathetic with Jim Vogel's struggle to gain his M.D., Pam had projected herself into a promised future. They would be married at the end of his internship; she would continue to help him financially while he worked out his years as a resident doctor.

Donna had been on hand when the crushing blow had come to her friend. Jim Vogel had flunked out of medical school months before Pam accidently discovered that fact. Confronted, he admitted that he had used Pam as a soft touch. The idealism that she had thought matched her own was a sham; Jim had been cruel enough to laugh at Pam's face-saving suggestion that one failure shouldn't discourage him. Couldn't he start all over? Pam was told, in the most callous terms, that medicine bored him; he had a new sales job. He had a new girlfriend, too. Would Pam please stop blubbering and get wise to herself?

Pam had survived the heartbreak and the humiliation, but she had not emerged unscarred. Afraid of exposing herself to another painful romance, she avoided prospective suitors and, in fact, drove interested men away with her aloof attitude. She had learned her lesson, she told Donna. She had learned it, Donna thought, too radically and too conclusively. Pam's life, already devoid of fun, was now insulated against love.

"People learn to hate you when you do too much for them," Pam Hollis said now. She got up to carry her coffee cup to the sink, placing it there carefully and without a sound.

To avoid further discussion, Donna admitted that possibility. Yet throughout the evening she remained haunted by her failure to reach Ann Julian, resenting Gar for two reasons now: one, because he was probably right, and, two, because Sunday night loomed dull and empty without a call from him.

FIVE

Ironically, Gar was present the next time Donna heard from Ann Julian.

With a minimum of warning, Gar had appeared at Donna's apartment door with a sackful of groceries in each arm, cheerfully announcing that he had found an irresistible bargain in T-bone steaks and was "perfectly willing to share them with any pretty nurses who would provide salt, pepper, and a broiler."

The impromptu dinner had been as enjoyable as it had been surprising, in spite of Pam's repeated protests that she was in the way. She insisted upon leaving the apartment before ten o'clock, although she was not due at the nearby hospital until eleven. Donna had visions of her friend sitting in a movie house or driving around aimlessly, killing time, all in the hope of encouraging romance, a commodity in which she herself had lost faith.

Gar's insistence, added to Donna's, went unheeded. And the door had no sooner closed behind Pam Hollis when the telephone rang.

"Competition?" Gar asked. He flashed his typical off-balance grin.

Donna laughed, crossing the room to the phone table. "Oh, sure. I may have to get an unlisted number, the way men call and call and call!"

Apart from having lunch with Dr. Janis the day before, Donna's social life had come to a standstill since her last date with Gar Breverman. His smile broadened; apparently Donna's facetious remark pleased him.

Donna lifted the receiver, genuinely puzzled by the late call. "Hello?"

"Miss Marker?" The youthful voice sounded strained. *"Donna?"*

"This is Donna, yes. Who . . . ?"

"Please come! He's choking! He can't get his breath!"

Donna had recognized the hysterical caller by then. "Who is it, Ann? What's wrong?"

"My brother. Come and help me . . . he's gonna die!"

41

"Can you get him to County? The emergency service . . ."

"No, no, no, he'll be dead! Oh, please, please!"

Gar was on his feet, aware that Donna was answering no ordinary call.

"It's the fastest way to get help, Ann."

"Come over . . . *hurry!*"

It was obvious that Ann was too terrified to follow logical advice. Whatever was wrong, valuable time was being wasted in arguing. "Where are you?" Donna asked.

"Twenty-six-eighty-four East Colton. Third floor." Ann's terror had made her almost incoherent. "Hurry! Willya? Hurry, please, *please!*"

"I'll be there in a few minutes," Donna said. "Try to stay calm. Don't frighten him." She dropped the receiver quickly. Gar was beside her as Donna raced for the door, repeating aloud the address Ann Julian had given her.

"What is it?" Gar demanded.

"I don't know. Can you drive, Gar? It's an emergency."

They ignored the elevator, running down the flight of stairs to the back of the apartment building, where Gar's Buick was parked. "Shouldn't we call a doctor?" Gar asked, his breath coming hard. "Ambulance?"

"She's too hysterical to tell me what's wrong. Just get me there, Gar. *Fast!*"

Twenty-six-eighty-four East Colton was a far cry from the gracious homes of Fairview where Ann Julian purportedly lived. Facing a railroad yard, on a street lined with dingy taverns, a pool hall, and a darkened pawnshop, the decrepit brick building rose four stories high, its innumerable compartments glaringly illuminated by unshaded light bulbs.

Gar Breverman and Donna climbed the three flights of steps anxiously, their nostrils assailed by a conglomeration of stale cooking odors, their ears assaulted by voices rising in shrill argument and the plaintive crying of a baby. The narrow wooden stairway, worn gray from years of haphazard wet-mopping, was lined with a hideous dark maroon and green wallpaper, its cabbage rose pattern peeling away in spots to reveal an equally depressing brown paint.

Ann was waiting for them in a doorway that opened onto the third floor stairwell, crying and clutching a boy of about six in her arms. Strangely, no neighbors had gathered; from behind other doors down the hall, a variety of blaring television channels kept the third-floor residents occupied.

Wordlessly, Gar and Donna followed Ann Julian into the apartment. Seconds later, with Ann's brother transferred to a garish royal blue plush sofa in the shabby living room, Donna established that the child was not choking on a foreign object; the ghastly noises and efforts to gulp a breath of air were symptoms of ordinary croup; terrifying symptoms to one who had never witnessed an attack, but a routine sight in hospital emergency rooms. The boy's strangulated sounds and his bluish complexion had turned even Gar pale.

"Is there a shower?" Donna asked crisply.

Ann nodded. She was sobbing too hard to reply with words.

"Hot water?"

A new wave of fear swept over Ann. "Wh-what are you going to do?"

Donna had scooped the child into her arms and was on her way to a small cubicle that passed as a bathroom. "Let him breathe some steam."

"Are you *sure?*" Gar seemed as dubious as the child's sister.

"Yes, I'm sure! We'll take him to County as soon as he gets his breath . . . get him some oxygen and a sedative. Turn on the hot water, Ann. Here, honey . . . I'm not going to hurt you." The boy grasped at Donna's arm,

44

caught in a paroxysm of choking, uttering half-wheezing, half-gutteral sounds.

Ann obeyed the order. A plastic shower curtain was wrapped around Donna and her frightened patient to shield them from the hot water, and the spigot was turned on. Seconds later, a cloud of steam filled the dirty, plaster-patched shower compartment, and Donna was encouraging the Julian boy to fill his lungs. "Atta boy! Take a *deep* breath now. Wa-ayy deep. *That's* the way! See . . . it's better now. Wa-a-y deep. Once more, honey. Now! You see? Better. That's *much* better!"

The unsophisticated effort worked a seeming miracle; in a matter of minutes the child's rasping efforts to inhale had been relieved and he was breathing normally. Leading the boy out of the steaming inferno of the bathroom, Donna watched Ann Julian grab her brother in her arms, more tearful now than she had been during the crisis.

"Oh, Timmy, Timmy . . . I was so scared! What happened? You okay now? Man, oh, man . . . if Ma'd been here, she'd of died!"

"I still want to take him to the hospital, Ann," Donna said gently.

Ann looked up, concerned. "Isn't he all right now?"

"I'm not a doctor, dear. Let's make sure,

hm? They'll let him inhale some oxygen and probably give him something to make sure he sleeps the rest of the night."

Gar was shaking his head, astounded by the sudden change. A few minutes ago, Timmy had looked as though he were dying. Now he appeared almost normal. "Whew! I'm still shaking! What the devil was *that* all about?"

"Croupy cough. Has he had a bad cold, Ann?"

"No. He had measles . . . sort of. Gosh, I dunno about the hospital. I mean, my mother's at the cleaning plant, and I don't have . . . any money in the house."

"There's no money involved, Ann. Remember that. If you ever have trouble again, even walking you're less than five minutes from the emergency room at County."

On the way to the hospital, Ann managed to get her tears under control, but she was deeply apologetic. "Man, I guess I did everything wrong. Timmy woke up and . . . boy, it was *awful*. All I could think about was to run downstairs and call you. Honest, I couldn't think of anything else to do. I guess it turned out all right, but . . . I mean, you wouldn't have gotten all shook up. You'd have known what to do, right off the bat."

"She spent a few years in school learning

46

what to do in an emergency," Gar pointed out. He parked the convertible near the hospital's emergency-service area, deciding to wait outside, unless Donna thought he'd be useful.

"I don't think we'll be long," Donna said. "Wait here, if you'd rather, Gar."

Less than fifteen minutes later, with Timmy no worse for his experience, Donna ushered Ann Julian and her brother through a night-hushed corridor of the hospital, toward a side exit. Outside a closed door marked "Volunteer Services," Ann came to an abrupt halt. On a bulletin board next to the door were tacked a variety of typewritten notices and schedules. But what had caught Ann's attention was a simply framed eight-by-ten photograph. "Hey, look!"

Donna turned back to examine the picture.

"Boy, they look about *my* age. Are those *nurses?*"

"Candy Stripers," Donna told her. "They do volunteer work, helping nurses."

"Oh, yeah? Around here?"

"In hospitals all over the country. They're teen-agers like yourself, Ann. Quite a few of them want to be nurses when they finish school. Not all of them."

"Cute outfits," Ann said, referring to the crisp, pinstriped pinafores. "They don't get paid, huh?"

"No."

"Just ... they just wanna help people? Is that it?"

"Help people and learn. Here at County there's a regular course for Candy Stripers, two evenings a week."

Ann frowned. "School?"

"Well, you have to learn hospital routine. You can't take on responsibilities without knowing what it's all about."

"Responsibilities like what?"

"Oh, helping with supplies. Seeing that the patients get their mail. Helping them with letters they want to write, or running errands for them. Or, maybe helping new patients get admitted. Even putting flowers in a vase properly takes a little know-how."

Ann continued to stare at the group photograph of perhaps a dozen attractive teen-aged girls who had recently earned the right to call themselves Candy Stripers.

"I guess they're all rich kids, huh? I mean, they don't have to have jobs after school, or anything. They can do all this charity jazz."

"They aren't all rich kids," Donna assured her. "Unless you want to figure that they're gaining valuable experience. A lot of them will go on into nursing careers with good backgrounds for the job."

Ann remained skeptical but interested.

48

"You have to have the loot to go through college."

"Not if you prove you're qualified. Nursing scholarships . . . If you have what it takes, you don't have to pay for your education."

Ann contemplated the picture for several more seconds. "They sure look cute. Must be a ball, getting to do a lot of important stuff in a neat place like this."

Donna agreed with the crude evaluation, expecting that the subject was closed. As they reached the door, Ann stopped Donna once more, this time by placing a timid hand on Donna's forearm. "Hey . . . before we get out there."

"Yes?"

Ann's eyes concentrated on the marble floor. "I guess you know that was a big line about . . . where I live and all that. It's a dump, where I live. My mother works in this dry-cleaning place. Pressing stuff. Nights."

"Your dad?"

Ann shrugged hopelessly. "Don't ask me. He used to drink a lot. I haven't seen him since Timmy was about two months old. I guess you must think I'm pretty scuzzy, tellin' you all that other stuff."

"We can forget about it, can't we?"

"Forget . . ."

"Pretend you never said any of it." Donna

smiled. "I've already forgotten what you said."

Ann sniffed, daubing at her face with the sleeve of a rather shabby red sweater. "Gee. You make me feel like two cents. I mean, you're so ... y'know ... *why would you wanna be nice to somebody like me?*" She thumbed her finger at Timmy. "Just about saved his life."

There was a brief, embarrassed silence, broken by Donna. "He's got to get home and get some sleep. Do you have the pills the doctor gave you?"

"I sure do. Boy, they were all so nice to us. Those two nurses and that doctor. I wish ..." Ann's small, pixielike face was lifted high for a moment, poised in wistful projection. "I wish I could do something neat like that for somebody." Almost ecstatically, she added, "For free, I mean. Not charge them one cent. Just ... *do* it. Y'know?"

Donna knew. As inarticulate and ungrammatical as Ann Julian might be, she had expressed the basic desire of all dedicated hospital personnel, and especially of volunteer medical aides. To be useful, to be wanted, to be appreciated, to be needed. Apart from Timmy, apparently no one had ever needed Ann's help. And, significantly, no one had a firmer hold on the girl's heart.

Drifting aimlessly, of no particular value to anyone except her brother, Ann seemed to have little regard for her own importance.

There was more than admiration for a chic uniform in her voice then, as Donna's new friend walked toward Gar Breverman's car and said, almost reverently, "Man, those girls sure looked sharp, didn't they?"

Perhaps she was comparing the immaculate Candy Stripers' uniform with the high-necked black sweater and tight black pants of the Tabby Cats, and all that each of the uniforms represented.

SIX

Although Gar Breverman had been more than cooperative in coming to Ann's rescue when help was needed, afterward he made it plain that he disapproved of Donna's involvement with the girl. At lunch the next day, he lectured her unmercifully on what he called "inexperienced meddling."

His reasoning infuriated Donna. "You mean you see something wrong with giving the kid a hand when she needs it? Letting her know that she has a few friends in the world?

51

I thought this was the whole basis for your work! Love. Showing people that they aren't rejected. Trying to help them!"

"You're talking about psychological approaches," Gar countered. "From a qualified counselor and within that person's immediate frame of reference. That girl needs a father, a mother who isn't out working all night and too exhausted to pay any attention to the kid all day. She needs –"

"Ann isn't lucky enough to have all that. That's why she turned to me."

"Exactly. They'll all turn to you in a pinch. And you'll find yourself so involved, so over your head in unsolvable problems, that you'll wear yourself out. And you'll get your heart broken, to boot. Not to mention doing a lot of possible harm."

"Harm?"

"Uh-huh. Expose that girl to a way of life she can't hope to have, under existing conditions. A smart apartment, pretty clothes . . ."

"I could help her change those conditions!" Donna cried.

"Sure. You can remodel the world, all with your tender little heart. Honey, you know the old saw about the road to hell being paved with good intentions? You're apt to place a big, unattainable, frustrating goal before

52

this kid. Keep inviting her over. When she wants the sharp furniture and clothes badly enough, she'll get them *her* way ... the only way her present social circle knows how to get anything. *Take* them. Because you know damned well she's not qualified to earn a good salary. And she's going to be influenced a good deal more by her Tabby Cat friends than by your exemplary life. Believe me!"

"You're telling me it's hopeless? You're supposed to be giving people in Ann's situation professional advice ... and you think they can't *ever* pull themselves up out of the mire?" Donna let her disgust override her desire to remain in Gar Breverman's good graces. "If you were honest, you'd admit you can't help anyone in this slum. You'd quit your job and open up a private practice, babying wealthy neurotics. You're ... *calloused!* You're downright *cruel*, if you get right down to it!"

"Sure. Why don't you tell me I'm *greedy?* That's why I'm working for the county on salary instead of getting twenty dollars an hour for my time. It's because I do care about people like Ann ..."

"That you resent driving a little boy to the hospital?"

Gar's anger had risen by now to match Donna's. "Don't twist my intentions. If that's all you think of me, fine! Forget you know me! I'm trying to make you understand a broad, serious social problem. I'm trying to make you see that driving a child to the hospital is one thing; mixing into Ann Julian's life is another. And you *are* mixing. Not just with Ann Julian. With her friends, her way of life. Just be sure you're equipped to handle the repercussions – that's all I'm trying to tell you."

"Why, she was as sweet and grateful . . ."

"Of course she was!" Gar exploded. "She's a human being! Look, you made me a promise . . ."

"I don't understand you," Donna said. "I don't know what you're driving at, objecting to, warning me against, criticizing me for . . ."

"That's your problem. You don't . . ."

"Oh, I don't have a Ph.D in psychology." Donna pronounced the words with scathing sarcasm. "It's all too *deep* for me. *I* can't use any of the fancy terminology *you* use. All I know is, Ann didn't come to you and your smug, up-in-the-clouds social workers when Timmy started choking. She called on a *friend*. Stupid little softhearted *me!*"

"Look who's calling who 'smug.' "

It was a hopeless, endless argument, and Gar cut it short by calling for the luncheon check. They left the drab little Colton Street café in cold silence, each convinced that the other was impenetrably stubborn, and with the unspoken but tacit understanding that they had no more to say to each other in the future.

Later, recalling the angry exchange and the icy separation, Donna gave way to private tears, but not to misgivings. She was right. How could there be any harm in befriending a pathetic, confused youngster? No amount of professional jargon from "experts" could shake that faith; she was absolutely right. Her only mistake had been in making that foolish promise to Gar. And perhaps the only way to win him back (for winning him back was a need more vital than playing the good Samaritan) was to *prove* to him that she was right.

Donna began her program to rehabilitate Ann Julian that evening, by dropping in at twenty-six-eighty-four East Colton. She remembered Gar's advice about not setting up impossible goals for her protégée. Didn't he know that there were gradual, possible goals?

Donna's revolution began with the Julian living quarters. She helped an astounded and then enthusiastic teenager clean the third-floor hovel from stem to stern.

She launched a seemingly hopeless home-beautifying campaign the next evening; used but attractive curtains from a neighborhood thrift shop covered windows that had probably never been washed before. A can of ten-cent-store-enamel revived a kitchen table, chairs, and a grocery shelf. Timmy's bed was painted and brightened with decals, and a windowsill bloomed with plastic geraniums. The thrift shop also yielded an apple-green shag rug and four picture frames for flower prints Donna cut from a magazine. Nothing that a home-decorating publication would have featured on its pages, but by the end of the week, a modern-day miracle to Ann and Timmy.

"Oh, man . . . it's so beautiful," Ann kept repeating.

"Wait'll Ma sees *this*, huh, Tim? It's like a . . . different place."

Most gratifying to Donna was Ann's attitude about the expenses involved. Minor expenses, to be sure; money that Donna would have spent without a second thought on cosmetics, a new record album, or a few extra pairs of nylons. But the principle involved (and Donna could almost sense Gar looking critically over her shoulder) was whether or not Ann was merely being helped, or being taught to help herself. Gratifyingly, the latter was true. "My mother feels the same way about it, Donna," Ann said. "I mean . . . we

56

don't want no . . . want *any* . . . like, charity. She says how much does she owe you?"

Donna had had only a fleeting encounter with Mrs. Julian. The evening before, on her way to work, Ann's mother had spoken to Donna for a few minutes, her tired voice barely audible. She was probably in her late thirties or early forties, but fatigue and a burdensome life had added another fifteen years to her appearance. Tiny, like Ann, she had the dark-ringed eyes and pallor of a consumptive; if she was not actually ill, she was certainly in need of a rest. Or perhaps it was only her embarrassment that made her speak in monosyllables, with her eyes cast to the ground. "The place was sure a mess. I used to try to keep it nice. I'm just so tired now . . . I guess I don't . . . care about anything, much. Just the kids get enough to eat."

Mrs. Julian neither lauded nor protested Donna's efforts at the time; she was late. Hers wasn't "much of a job," but the boss was "pretty nice, if you don't get there late." Apparently her show of pride had been reserved for a private conversation with Ann. How much did she owe?

"It's just a few dollars," Donna said.

"I don't care. You did all this work – we wanna pay for the rug and stuff."

57

They reached a compromise that would have won Gar's approval. (Always that eagerness to please Gar, although he had managed to avoid Donna since the argument.) Donna had a number of nylon uniforms that needed pressing; she'd be wearing them now that the weather was warmer. If Ann wanted to earn the money spent on "redecorating" . . .

Ann did. She wanted more than that. After Timmy had been tucked into bed, over cups of hot chocolate served in the brightly painted kitchen corner, Ann said abruptly. "If I get this scaggy hair cut and fixed real cute, and if I could do my homework during study period, I know one thing I'd like."

"What's that, Ann?"

"I'd like to be one of those . . . what do you call them?" She smiled unexpectedly; during the past week she had occasionally laughed out loud over some minor mishap with a paintbrush or needle and thread, but usually when she talked about herself, she was painfully serious. Now she was amused by her own error. "I always start to call them *Peppermint* Stripers. Anyway, I'd sure like that."

Donna's hopes soared. She felt almost righteously smug. "You'd like to be a Candy Striper?"

"Man, why not? Learn all that important

58

stuff and work up to a real job. I guess I told you? I'd like to be a nurse." More emphatically, Ann added, "I'd like to be exactly like you!"

Their enthusiasm was short-lived. Classes for volunteers at County Hospital were held two evenings a week.

"Evenings," Ann said dejectedly. "That's all, man. I can't go out nights."

In one sense, Mrs. Julian's nighttime job was a blessing in disguise; it kept Ann at home, babysitting, with a legitimate excuse not to join the Tabby Cats' "special activities." For all Donna knew, the after-dark confinement had not only kept Ann off the streets but out of juvenile court. Still, if a daytime job could be found for Mrs. Julian, perhaps a job that was less physically demanding, during Timmy's school hours . . . or if Timmy could spend some of his day in the McKittrick Day Nursery . . .

Donna decided the risk might be worthwhile. But, methodically (as Gar would do it), she asked a pointed question. "What if we could swing it so that your mother's at home nights, Ann? On Tuesdays and Thursdays you'd take the Candy Stripers' course. That only lasts about six weeks. Then you'd probably be assigned to one evening a week doing volunteer work. That leaves you with six evenings free."

"Yeah, but I have homework, don't I? From regular school?" Ann looked about her at the renovated flat. "I wouldn't want all this to go to pot, either. I mean, you have to keep a place up, if you want it to look cute."

Donna fixed her with a level stare. "What about your club, Ann?"

It was a humiliating reminder. "Oh ... that."

"Yep. 'Oh, *that.*' Would you drop Tabby and the other girls?"

Ann's fingers dug into the linoleum table cover, her eyes avoiding Donna's. "Gee ... in a way ... they're sort of ... well, they're friends of mine. We have this secret pledge, like if one of us gets in trouble, all the other kids have to stand up for you. Like a ... sorority, see? We ..."

"Suppose you aren't going to be *getting* into any trouble?"

"I dunno. It's rough. The kids don't like it when you fink out. It's like you think you're too good for them or something. Y'know? They hold it against you. I remember one time this girl – Tina, her name was ..."

Ann cut her story off at that point, refusing to be coaxed into revealing what had happened to Tina, who had very likely resigned from Tabby Cat membership. Ann held fast to her stand: she had no desire to "hang around the park" with the gang, but there was a matter of "loyalty."

Donna broke down the resistance based on pure honor. "You're afraid to drop out, aren't you?"

Ann was silent for a few moments, her silence heavy with misery. Finally, in a hoarse whisper, she said, "You'd have to . . . sort of . . . *ease* out. Make excuses and show up less and less. I guess that's what you'd have to do. You can't just . . . tell the kids you don't want nothing – *anything* – to do with them. Nobody likes that, do they? You just . . . drop 'em like so much garbage?" Having justified her point, at least to her own satisfaction, Ann looked up at Donna beseechingly. "I could do it, though. You wouldn't have to worry. I don't want trouble. I wasn't ever with them when they . . . like, roughed up somebody in the park, or went out on a rumble with the Conquests. They even carried broken bottles and chains under their sweaters when the guys had a fight with some other gang. If a guy from the Valiants, say, tried to get fresh with a Tabby Cat, there'd be this big rumble they set up, and Tabby would get us girls . . . only I wasn't ever there because of Timmy . . . she'd get the girls to bring the weapons. That way, if the guys got nabbed,

61

the cops wouldn't find a knife or anything on them . . ."

Donna shuddered inwardly as the recital went on. And Ann must have had need for this verbal catharsis; she revealed more about the local teen-age activities, male and female, than her so-called pledge of honor could possibly have permitted. More than she could have known if she had never participated. More, much more, than Donna cared to hear.

By the time Ann had detailed a number of spine-chilling "club projects," she had evidently begun to hear them through Donna's ears. She was, or so it seemed to Donna, seeing the Tabby Cats as society saw them: purposeless, vicious, dangerous. Pathologic. And pitiful. "I'll quit. I'll get out," Ann promised. In the next sentence she dismissed the gang as though it didn't exist: "Could Miss Hollis do what she said she would? Y'know . . . cut my hair and fix it up kind of casual . . . more like yours?"

"If Pam offered to do something, I'm sure she meant it," Donna said. "Let's wait and see what we can work out."

There seemed to be no doubt in Ann's mind that her friend would work the miracle. Donna left her talking excitedly about County

Hospital, and, most exciting of all, belonging to a different kind of gang – the teen-agers who wore "peppermint stripes."

SEVEN

Donna returned to her own apartment after ten o'clock that evening, totally unprepared for the sound of a male voice coming from behind her door.

For a few hopeful seconds she thought that the unheralded visitor might be Gar. But before she turned the doorknob, Donna recognized the voice as belonging to Walter Janis.

Dr. Janis and Pam greeted her effusively, with almost too much enthusiasm to be sincere, Donna suspected. Her chief seemed to feel that it was necessary to explain his presence:

"I . . . worked late tonight – I guess you know I wanted to reorganize the exam room. And after dinner, I thought . . . since I'm only a few blocks away, why not stop by and visit with Donna?"

He sounded almost childish, making the explanation. As though he had been caught in an awkward situation and an excuse was forthcoming.

Pam Hollis was equally uneasy. "We've really been waiting for you, Donna. But we ... got to talking. Dr. Janis had thought about specializing in surgery. Did you know that?"

"Yes," the doctor embellished. "Before I decided babies were more fascinating than old gall bladder patients. I'm still intrigued by surgery. Pam's been telling me about some interesting new developments in the field."

Donna made one of her hasty surveyals and followed it with an equally quick conclusion. Walter Janis may have come to call on her, but he had struck pay dirt in finding Pam home alone. That they had enjoyed the past few hours together, that they had found a myriad of subjects in common, and that Donna's coming home had interrupted an exciting rapport all seemed too obvious for comment. It was like walking in on a closed conference, or finding yourself intruding upon a honeymoon. No, not actually *that* uncomfortable. But almost. Donna found herself wishing she had spent another hour at the Julians' flat.

Urged to join the conversation, she told Walter Janis and Pam about the most recent development in her project. "Ann wants you to fix her hair, Pam. She's smart enough to know you can't run around a hospital with that long, gypsy-style hairdo."

Pam and the doctor were impressed. They discussed Donna's rehabilitation project and agreed that it was a wonderful gesture on her part.

Before Pam had to leave for the hospital, Donna concluded that her roomie and her boss were not only appreciative of her work with a confused tenement-house teen-ager; they were grateful for it. If it had not been for Ann Julian, Donna would have been at home this evening. Being out, she had unwittingly spurred a budding relationship between a doctor who loved his work so much that he had lost his love and a nurse who had loved a man so much that she had turned to her work as a refuge from heartbreak.

Pam Hollis and the doctor! They formed a logical combination, Donna thought. And if they continued to see each other (which appeared certain), Donna would take pride, in the future, for bringing them together.

But tonight their engrossment with each other, and the quick, warm bond that had formed between them, only intensified a loneliness that could not be dispelled by a minor success with a floundering youngster.

Donna fell asleep that night wondering first

what Gar would think of her progress with
Ann Julian. After a while, Ann faded from
the picture, and Gar's professional opinion
became less important. Pam, Walter, Ann
... finding a suitable daytime job for Mrs.
Julian ... all drifted off into obscurity and
unimportance. Gar Breverman alone was the
issue. Not his theories, nor his irritating
criticisms. Just Gar. Being with him. Having
him near. Being loved by him.

EIGHT

If Ann Julian had expected miracles of Donna,
the miracles were more than doubled as she
justified Donna's efforts in her behalf.

First, there had been a long talk with
Mrs. Julian, digging into her past experience
and her qualifications for a less strenuous
job. Donna had gathered her information
methodically, and then, during a lunch hour,
marched across the street to confer with
an old friend, Mrs. Hale, the nurse who
supervised the Admitting Office at County
Hospital.

No, there wasn't any need at this time for a
filing clerk in Admitting, but the Accounting

Office was screaming for help in that department. "Let me call Juanita upstairs," Mrs. Hale said, reaching for the telephone. Minutes later, Mrs. Julian's employment interview was arranged. Two days later, Ann's mother had left her steam-clouded night job in the cleaning plant to accept a clerical job at the hospital. The starting salary was only a shade lower than her previous earnings, and fringe benefits and a schedule of early promotions promised a better return.

"I know people ought to move upward on their own initiative," Donna told Pam Hollis afterward. "Sometimes they get too beat out to even think about improving their lot."

Pam understood that perfectly. "You get into a rut," she agreed. "You need someone else to come along and give you a shove in the right direction."

Pam was well qualified to speak on that subject. While the improvement in Mrs. Julian's situation had been preplanned, her own "shove in the right direction" had been purely accidental. What a fluke of luck it had been to have Dr. Janis find himself with time on his hands! And what manna from heaven it had been to have Donna out of the apartment long enough for the visitor to strike up an immediate bond of understanding with the recluse! Pam was more than grateful; she was ecstatic. In three weeks she had not spent one evening or one day off without Walter Janis for company.

Donna's campaign extended itself to the day nursery at the settlement house. Timmy Julian was old enough to go to school; the free child-care service was intended for preschoolers. Besides, they were filled up, and there couldn't possibly be room for another youngster, even if it was only from two-thirty until four.

Donna cajoled, pleaded, persisted, and threatened to make an "impossible pest of herself."

Nancy Bellows, in charge of the nursery, slapped her forehead in mock despair. "You already *have*, Donna." Nancy's sigh was genuine. "I don't know where we'll put him, but let's get him registered. And no more! Understand? You can stand on your head next time, but this is *it*."

Donna hugged her impulsively and filled out Timmy's card. Ann Julian was free to join a new kind of "gang."

By the end of Ann's second week in the Candy Stripers' class at County, the supervising nurse (a member of Donna's own graduating class) made a glowing report: "Ann's a bit crude in her grammar, and we're working on that," Helen Vernon said. "But she's going at it as though the hospital would fold up if she didn't do everything exactly right."

"She's really working, then?"

"I just told you, Donna. She's almost too deadly serious. I'm beginning to get self-conscious about my own weaknesses. She's going to make one dilly of a head nurse someday."

"If you can get her to stop saying 'man' before every sentence." Donna laughed, immensely pleased with the prediction.

Helen Vernon laughed, too. "Man, I wouldn't want to be working *for* her. Ann's going to grow up into one of those Medical Machines in White. The perfectionist kind that make probies shiver in their oxfords."

In four weeks, Donna found herself without a project; with the Julian family squared away, she lacked an outlet for her extra energy, and the hours after she finished her work at the clinic weighed heavily on her hands. There was more time now to miss Gar, to regret the silly, abstract argument that separated them.

With Pam Hollis either out on a date with Dr. Janis or monopolizing the conversation by raving abut his sterling qualities, Donna found herself bereft of an opportunity to crow a bit about her accomplishment. But, though she missed the long talks with Pam, she was delighted with the distraction that had changed their dull routine. Besides, Pam had already given her full credit for making a radical change for the better in the Julian family. It was Gar from whom she wanted the acknowledgment. Not to say, "I told you so." Just to ... have him know that his dire predictions had proved to be wrong. To have him know that his purposes and her own were entirely compatible. Or, failing that, just to have his approval again, on any grounds.

Near the end of May, Donna found herself alone one afternoon in the clinic's outer office. A cancelled appointment and a run of unusually cooperative babies had resulted in an equally unique rest break.

"You'd think crying babies were going out of style," the doctor said. "Did you notice this morning? Three shots in absolute silence."

"Did I *notice!* Wasn't it heaven?"

"I charmed them," Walter said.

Donna smiled. "They were probably dead-end kids. Didn't feel a thing."

"That's right, Nurse. Deflate my ego. A really good pediatrics nurse goes around assuring the doctor that he has an irresistible way with babies."

Donna checked the appointment sheet and pulled a card out of the desk file. "You'll have a chance to prove it pretty soon, Doctor. Baby

Ramirez. He's a yeller."

"He sticks up for his rights," Walter Janis conceded. "I don't believe in discouraging a fighting spirit."

"Baby Ramirez comes *in* yelling," Donna remembered.

"He's consistent. He goes out yelling, too. What's more, he doesn't do much for my nerves while I'm checking him over." The doctor crossed over to look beyond the screen door into the bleak side street. "This is a strange building, isn't it? Eight different departments, all under one roof, and each one isolated from the other. We go weeks without seeing anyone from Recreation or Counseling."

Weeks without even a glimpse of Gar Breverman, Donna thought; he came to work half an hour after she did, and usually left later. Worked two evenings a week, too. He might as well be in the Congo as separated from the pediatrics clinic by a dingy wall.

It was better to say nothing, Donna thought, than to reveal her misery. She could conceive of no comment that wouldn't, somehow, involve Gar's name.

Ironically, Walter Janis made the reference for her. "It's ridiculous. Here I work just a few feet away from Gar Breverman, and I think the last time I saw him was . . . oh,

71

six weeks ago at the lunch place around the corner. And last night, with all the restaurants to choose from downtown, Pam and I run into him at The Branding Iron."

"Oh?"

"Didn't Pam tell you?"

"I don't get to talk to her mornings. She's asleep when I leave the house."

"We had a drink together, matter of fact. He was with Nancy. You know Nancy Bellows . . . over in the day nursery?"

Donna nodded. She not only knew Nancy; she owed her a favor. Not only knew her, but recognized her as an exceptionally attractive, warmly accommodating person. Nancy was too busy with her job to meddle in affairs that would be more "properly" handled by psychologists, sociologists, and juvenile officers. Nancy was too sweet to argue; she would sit at a dinner table and listen to Gar with respect, if not downright awe. Unlike Baby Ramirez . . . and Donna Marker . . . she wasn't a yeller who stood up for her rights.

Nancy was, in fact, exactly the kind of girl Gar Breverman would fall in love with. And it was no consolation at all, when your insides were churning with jealousy, to be unable to find one solitary fault with your rival. A pretty girl, a pleasant girl, a generous and intelligent girl; *one who kept her promises.*

72

Donna realized suddenly that the doctor was still talking to her. "Nancy's quite impressed with you, you know."

"*Me?*"

"Yes, she was telling us all about the little Julian boy and his sister – I think the girl picks him up at the nursery when she gets out of high school – isn't that right?"

"Yes . . . about this time," Donna said.

"I believe the girl's told Nancy all about what you've done for her . . . for the whole family, actually. Nancy didn't have to give you quite such a glowing build-up. After all, she was talking to three people who think a lot of you already. But she certainly couldn't have said more complimentary things about you."

Gar had heard, then. He knew all about the success of the Julian project, but he hadn't stopped by this morning to offer congratulations. Maybe he was disgruntled because his advice had been ignored – with excellent results. Or perhaps he was simply too interested in the girl who had told the story to bother with "amateur do-gooders."

Donna felt a wave of deep depression sweep over her. Especially in remembering that she *had* seen Pam Hollis this morning. Usually, Pam got home at seven-fifteen and was dead to the world when Donna rose at seven-thirty.

This morning Pam had been delayed at the hospital, and she had arrived at the apartment in time to join Donna at the breakfast table. Pam had talked briefly about her date the night before ... even to a description of the charcoal-broiled steaks at The Branding Iron. But Pam hadn't mentioned seeing Gar with another girl. Typically, Pam had been considerate. It only added to Donna's misery to know that her feelings were being spared.

Dr. Janis started toward the examining room nearest the office. "Heard a lot about some of our neighbors' problems last night, too. Nancy's department – overcrowded and understaffed. The counselors up to their necks trying to straighten out problems I couldn't even imagine, to say nothing of tackling. . . ."

There was a shrill cry from somewhere outside the building. Dr. Janis came hurrying back into the office as Donna started toward the screen door. "What was that?"

"I don't know. Kids whooping it up, probably." Donna peered down the narrow street. "I don't see . . ." Before she finished the sentence the shriek was repeated, and someone came around the corner, running, half stumbling toward the door. In the same instant that she realized it was Ann Julian, Donna saw the reason for the girl's panic: the

74

trio chasing her, yelling like banshees, were in no playful mood.

"*Donna . . . let me in!*"

Donna responded to the terrified plea instantly, pushing open the screen door. Ann rushed into the room, nearly colliding with Dr. Janis in her frenzied effort to reach a sanctuary.

"What's going on here?" Donna shouted. The doctor joined her in the open doorway, their backs shielding Ann.

Apparently Donna's anger, and the presence of two adults blocking the entrance, had a sobering effect on the feminine rat pack. Or perhaps the medical uniforms did the trick: From what Donna had learned, Tabby Lacer was not above knocking down anyone who stood in her way, but she retained a conditioned fear of authority, even though she lacked respect for law. She stopped several feet from the clinic doorway, breathless, examining Donna and Dr. Janis with a smirking contempt. The plump girl she called Jo-Jo and the reptile-eyed redhead named Nicki came to a halt, too.

"I asked you a question!" Donna said sharply. "What do you think you're doing?"

"Tell your finky friend to step out here. I'll show her what." Tabby lifted a hand and looked significantly at her clawlike

75

fingernails. The flunkies behind her snickered their appreciation. Somewhere behind Donna, Ann Julian had started up a muffled sobbing.

"I don't know what it's all about," Walter Janis announced. "But I won't have disturbances here. If you girls have no business here, get . . ."

"Oh, we *have* business here," Tabby said with poisonous sweetness. "We're waitin' fer a friend a mine." There were more sycophantic titters. "Ain't that right?"

"You know it," Jo-Jo said.

The redhaired girl lifted a corner of her mouth in a vicious half-smile. "Yeah"

"You'd better get going," the doctor insisted. His voice was firm, but entirely too mild in tone to impress the trio in black.

"What's your hurry, Doc?"

"We ain't in no hurry."

"Yeah. We got time."

"Hey, Julian! C'mon out . . . we wanna *talk* to ya!"

"Yeah! Ya a *baby* or somethin', ya gotta see a baby doc?" Jo-Jo guffawed over her own attempt at humor.

Nicki licked her lips, tugged at her phoney leopardskin vest, and muttered, "She's chicken."

Seething inside, Donna turned to Walter Janis. "Maybe I'd better call the police."

76

"I think so," he agreed. "Go ahead."

Astoundingly, the loudest reaction came from Ann. "No, don't do that! Don't call the cops!" She was clinging to Donna's arm, looking more frightened now than when she had rushed into the office. "They'll *never* leave me alone if you do that."

"Well, you certainly can't hide here for the rest of your life!" Donna said irritably.

"This is a *clinic!*" the doctor shouted, probably as much for Ann's benefit as for the gang's. "We're expecting patients ... we can't have this sort of thing going on!"

Seething with anger, Donna turned back toward the doorway. "Why don't you find something useful to do instead of acting like savages? Aren't you ashamed of yourselves?"

Donna's impassioned cry resulted in utter frustration. Tabby and her Cats looked coolly amused, eyeing Donna as though she were a ridiculous insect that had made a noise, attracted their attention momentarily, and upon closer surveillance barely merited their contempt.

Worse than the humiliation of being ignored was looking beyond the girls to see Gar Breverman. He was shaking his head apparently in disbelief as much as disgust. And suddenly Donna was hearing her words through his ears. *"Aren't you ashamed of yourselves?"* Silly words, revealing her abysmal lack of experience and her naïveté! She might as well have faced a murderous mob and whispered, *"Please* behave yourselves. Be nice!"

Fortunately, Gar's silent criticism didn't go beyond that first incredulous gesture. Donna watched him walk over to Tabby's side – to mutter something into the blonde leader's ear. Tabby shot him a look that could have been pure arsenic. Gar spoke to the girl for another few seconds, keeping his voice down so that Donna could not hear his words. Whatever he said, although the reaction was far from being friendly, he got results. Tabby Lacer made a "let's-go" sign with her head and turned around, her balloon-shaped hairdo rocking in time with her purposeful movements as she made her way across the street. Like attached puppets, Jo-Jo and Nicki followed, their movements lazy and sullen. Like coyotes slinking away, Donna thought; dispersed but not vanquished. Sooner or later they would be back.

Gar came to the open doorway, repeating the same question Donna and Dr. Janis had asked moments before: "What was *that* all about?" His quick glance took in Ann Julian and he arrived at his own answer. "Giving her a hard time, eh?"

"I ... came to get my kid brother," Ann whimpered. "They were outside the nursery. . . ."

"I'm surprised it hasn't happened sooner," Gar said. He looked toward Donna meaningfully. "You knew it would, didn't you?"

Ann had gotten her tears under control, though she was shivering now like a gun-shy pup at a firing range. "It's not just ... dropping out. That's not why Tabby's mad." Perceptively, she had caught the psychologist's intimation, and now she rallied to Donna's defense. "You think it's just 'cause Donna made me quit runnin' around with those kids?"

"That's a pretty sound assumption," Gar replied.

Walter Janis seemed to have tired of the whole affair; with no further threat of disturbance, he returned to his examining room, calling back, "I'll let you experts handle it. I lose interest in kids after they're two years old."

The doctor's interruption was unfortunate. Ann seemed to lose her train of thought, and Gar didn't press her for details. If Ann had intended to absolve Donna from blame, her explanation for the gang's attack was now forgotten.

"We'd better get you home," Gar said.

Ann started out the door. "I'm sure sorry this had to happen, Donna. Tell Dr. Janis I'm sorry too." Embarrassed, she added, "I always run to you for help, don't I?"

Donna resisted an urge to repeat the old, trite reminder that "that's what friends are for." Besides, she was still too shaken by the experience, and too self-conscious in Gar's presence, to risk saying anything that might sound foolish to him.

"I . . . have to get Timmy," Ann said. "My brother . . . he's around the corner."

"At the day nursery," Donna explained. Hastily – impulsively – as always. She cursed herself mentally in the next instant.

"Yes, I know," Gar said. "I've seen him there." He smiled at Ann Julian, handing her an immaculate white handkerchief. "Blot up, Annie. You don't want Tim and Miss Bellows seeing you all soggy." He patted Ann's shoulder affectionately. "I have a short break now. I'll drive you kids home."

Ann turned to thank Donna once more. She seemed reluctant to go with Gar, and her expression asked dozens of silent questions; she was safe now, but what about tomorrow? She couldn't walk from school to the settlement-house nursery, from her home to the hospital, without fearing another attack.

80

Next time there might not be an open door to run to, or a protector to convoy her home. Wouldn't she pay dearly for this privilege? In the teen-age code, you settled differences without appealing to the authorities for assistance. What about *tomorrow?* Fear shone like a fierce light in the wide brown eyes, and though Ann wiped her tears away, her brave attempt at a smile failed pitifully.

Gar's farewell was a perfunctory, "I'll see that she gets home. Nice seeing you again, Donna."

Donna watched the pair until they had rounded the corner, headed for Nancy Bellow's department. Then, swallowing hard to ward off the threat of incipient tears, she joined Dr. Janis in the adjoining room.

Although he had been somewhat tactless earlier, mentioning Gar's date with another girl, Walter Janis was not completely insensitive. And it was only natural that Pam had talked to him. At any rate, he sounded sympathetic as he asked, "How did it go?"

"Go?"

"You haven't seen Gar in quite a while. What I meant was . . ." He grinned, looking a little sheepish about prying into Donna's private life. "I meant . . . was there any . . . *progress?*"

"If that's asking me if he made a date to see me again," Donna replied, "the answer is no." She busied herself for a few moments covering the examining table with clean linen. "No progress, Doctor."

Dr. Janis was genuinely sorry: Donna knew that from the somber way in which he said, "I got out of the way, hoping something encouraging might happen."

Donna managed a weak smile. "I guess, under the circumstances, something encouraging *did* happen."

"Oh, really? I thought you said . . ."

"He actually remembered my name!"

NINE

Gar remembered more than Donna's name; he remembered to stop in at the pediatrics clinic just before closing time to report that Ann and Timmy had gotten home safely.

"I gather she doesn't go to County tonight," Gar added.

"No. She has a class there tomorrow evening, though." Donna frowned, acutely uncomfortable under Gar's penetrating stare. It was like having an all-knowing demigod

82

standing over your desk; worshiping him silently, you were nonetheless aware that none of your human weaknesses escaped him. "She'll spend tonight at home, but . . ."

"She'll have to walk to school tomorrow morning," Gar said. His calm voice, considering Donna's own agitation, was infuriating. "She'll have to come back here after school tomorrow, too."

"I know what you want me to say. She can't have a bodyguard assigned to her."

"No," Gar said evenly. "No, she can't. She's on her own."

Donna slammed a note pad onto the desk. "What are you trying to do, convince me that there's no law and order left? Someone's got to look after Ann. The police . . . someone! We aren't living in a *jungle!*"

Gar sighed and dropped into one of the plastic waiting-room chairs near the door. "We've finally come to the root of our disagreement, Donna. Correction. East Colton Street district *is* the jungle."

Donna caught her breath. It lodged in her throat, reflecting her tension. It was a tension born of the sudden realization that Gar was probably right; obscure as his earlier reasoning might have sounded, he had probably been right all along!

"The jungle," Gar repeated quietly. "In

which domesticating the rabbit does not enhance his chances of escaping being devoured by the tiger."

Defensively now, Donna asked, "What do you propose? Turning the rabbits into tigers? Is that the marvelous solution you have for Ann? If a decent girl finds herself forced to live here, what advice do you give her? Tell her to practice being meaner? Tougher? Twice as vicious as Tabby Lacer?"

"If you'll calm down a second, I'll try to tell you what we're *trying* to do," Gar said. Donna's outburst had left his completely unruffled, and his self-control served as a maddening contrast to her anger. "We're working with closely bound units within that jungle society. We'd *like* to wean the hopefuls, like Ann, away from the gang. It would work beautifully if we could rehabilitate these kids one by one and let them start all over in a fresh milieu. Trouble is, they're stuck right here, at least until they're self-supporting. And what happens when we break them out of that familiar orbit? We kindle resentments in the gang . . . justifiable resentments, if you . . ."

"*Justifiable?* Those wildcats this afternoon . . ."

"*If,*" Gar persisted, "if you see the world through their eyes."

"But you know those girls are wrong."

"I said 'if you see the world through their eyes,' Donna! You can't. You're being rational, sensible, moral, and just. All within *your* frame of reference. Not Tabby's."

Donna leaped to her feet. "Is that your standard? Tabby's opinion of what's right and wrong? Ann told me plenty about her. She's sadistic. She's dishonest. She . . ."

"She's the leader," Gar said. "We begin by trying to reach *her*."

"But you can't! She's like a . . . hardened criminal. You once said yourself that some of the girl gangs are worse than . . ."

"Donna?"

"You know that's true!"

"Donna, *she's seventeen years old.* Her father's a fist-happy drunk and her mother free-lances, off and on, with a string of sordid characters. Tabby's been locked out of her own home for hours at a time since she was four years old. While Mama . . . Lord knows what she's doing! I could go on. It's not a pretty story, but we know every detail of it. And if Tabby's mad at the world, she may have a few reasons to be."

"What have you done about it?"

Gar rose slowly from his chair. "You want a simple, black and white answer, don't you?"

"Have you ever tried doing what I did with Ann? Offering her affection? Showing her the

85

world's got people in it who don't beat you up while they're drunk, and don't turn your home into a brothel? People who care?"

Gar walked to the desk, picking up a pencil and toying with it as he spoke. "Before you start congratulating yourself on your success with Ann, get this straight. Ann might have been economically underprivileged and emotionally deprived. Her mother might have ignored her, but she ignored her out of exhaustion ... sometimes out of despondency. What Ann knew right along, though, is that she wasn't hated. Nobody who works all night over a steam iron so that you can be fed despises you."

"Mrs. Julian doesn't ..."

"I know. You found her a better job. Wonderful. I'm not being sarcastic ... I mean that. What I'm trying to tell you is that Ann wasn't a hard-core delinquent. She got swept into the gang – she didn't organize it."

"All right, then. Tabby's hard core. So she needs twice as much understanding. She needs love."

"From you?" Gar asked. "From me?"

Donna hesitated. Tabby was eons removed from being lovable. "I suppose so. Yes. From ... anyone."

"In seventeen years of being kicked around, you learn to kick back. You kick first, before the other guy kicks you. That's Tabby's orientation. She wears an emotional armor plate thicker than that wall over there." Gar thumbed at the wall separating the room from his own offices. "And it has a sign on it, Donna. 'Adults Keep Out.' Especially adults with authority. Parents, teachers, police officers, counselors. . . ."

A nurse wouldn't count, Donna thought. A baby nurse, with no authority and no interest except perhaps a personal one. It could be done. With patience and understanding, Tabby could be reached. Not as easily as Ann, but she could be reached. Aloud, Donna said, "Everyone wants to be liked . . . or loved. Tabby's no exception. She's capable of love, too. Every girl is. At seventeen . . ."

"She's capable," Gar admitted. "In fact, Chip O'Neill is our one hope of getting past that hard shell."

"Who?"

"Chip. He leads a gang of his own."

"Oh yes. The . . . Conquests."

"You've been learning," Gar said. "Well, he's *it*. Tabby's soft spot. Her Achilles' heel."

"Some soft spot. A hoodlum."

"Uh-uh. A mixed up kid. Impressionable and, from my contacts with him, vulnerable. I'm treating two members of his family. We have contact." Gar moved toward the door.

"It's a case of starting at the top, Donna. Not at the bottom, with the easy ones who only get hurt in the process. At the top. Trying to reroute *that* energy. You see, Donna, we haven't had much success weaning individuals from gangs. And we haven't done too well breaking up the gangs. But we've managed to keep a few gangs intact and turn them into positive channels."

"Words, words, words! I wouldn't know how to tackle a whole gang," Donna said. "All I know is, Ann's making her mark across the street. She's become a whiz at arranging flowers. You ought to see patients light up when she walks into a room!"

Gar opened the door. "I shouldn't wonder. She's a charming kid."

That infuriating superiority! That cool, officious dismissal of someone else's success, when all he had to offer were theories and hopes and possibilities for a far-off future!

"Isn't that better than carrying switchblades and broken bottles to Colton Park?"

"Much better," Gar agreed. "In another few months, she might have had company. If the wall between us and the Tabby Cats hadn't widened."

"You're talking about a pipe dream . . . months from now. I'm talking about Ann Julian *today*."

"She's fine today," Gar said. His eyes bored deeply into Donna's for an instant. "Cross your fingers she'll be as lucky tomorrow. Good night."

Donna vaguely remembered muttering some sort of response. She heard the door close behind Gar, felt the sudden, overpowering emptiness of the room.

He was gone, and she had wasted the time with him once again, raking over the pros and cons of a situation that probably concerned them more than it did the subjects. Ann was probably deep in dinner or homework by now. Tabby and her gang might have sauntered over to the park to see what they could stir up in the way of "action"; none of them could have cared less about a silly, overidealistic nurse who had tackled the jungle and fallen in love with the Great White Hunter.

Why couldn't she have nodded, looked at Gar with simple adoration, and admitted that he knew more about Colton Street's juvenile misfits than she ever wanted to know?

Disgust with herself and worry over Ann Julian haunted Donna as she locked the clinic door after herself shortly after five. Dr. Janis had left early, making a discreet exit minutes after Gar had come in. Now there was no one in sight, though the psychological counseling offices next door were still open; Gar had mentioned appointments this evening.

Crossing the street to the almost deserted parking area, Donna felt a vague queasiness. The daylight would last for another three hours, but the stillness, broken only by a scrap metal truck rattling down Colton Street, gave the effect of night. Gauging her reaction more accurately, Donna realized that she felt completely alone. Though she had walked across the walled-in lot many times in the winter darkness, she had never experienced this sensation of aloneness in an alien place.

It was not fear that accelerated her breath. Donna reassured herself that it *couldn't* be fear. Why now, when she had walked this same neighborhood time and again as a student nurse, completely assured that her uniform protected her like a coat of mail? Who would wish to harm a person devoted to aiding the sick and helpless? One who had voluntarily chosen service to the least fortunate, when she could as easily have chosen to be a special-duty nurse, earning fat fees as the traveling companion for some wealthy hypochondriac? The white uniform was both a pledge and a protection; Donna had always prided herself in the respect it commanded. Why did she feel less secure now? Why, as she neared the few cars still parked in the lot, did she make a broad detour? To avoid someone who might be lurking behind them? Was it the talk of "the jungle" that had stirred this uneasiness? Maybe it was remembering those three imperturbable, grotesquely painted faces, in which she had searched vainly for some glimmer of warm response, some hope of human understanding. There had been none. Tabby, Nicki, and Jo-Jo – three false names and three faces that might have been caricature masks. There had been no respect for Dr. Janis, for what his skill and knowledge and devotion meant to their community. With just the smallest additional provocation, Donna was now certain, they would have thought nothing of resorting to physical violence.

Why? What made them so lacking in compassion, so deliberately eager to demonstrate their rebellion with force? Were they born without conscience or a sense of fair play? Three of them chasing a tiny slip of a girl down a narrow dead-end street! Why? Because she had tried to better her life, to escape the cage of hatred in which they themselves were imprisoned. What would they have done if Ann had not escaped from them?

Donna's hand was trembling when she finally reached out to unlock her car, yet she experienced an enormous sense of relief when the motor started quickly and the Chevy (its door locked from the inside for the first time) hurried her out of the parking lot and toward the brightly lighted street.

There was a second surge of relief, this time mingled with hope and gratitude, as Donna drove past the settlement-house building. Silhouetted in the open doorway to the counseling offices, she saw a familiar figure. How long Gar Breverman had been standing there she did not know, but she was reasonably certain that when she had walked from the clinic door to her car she had not really been completely alone.

Steuben's Drugstore, occupying a corner across the street from Colton Park, was as crowded as ever. Donna had made the stop impulsively, backing her car into the first parking space that presented itself once she had made her decision: Pam and Dr. Janis were going out to dinner, and cooking dinner for yourself alone was a smashing bore; why not a plate lunch and malt at Steuben's counter?

Surrounded by equally lonely strangers, Donna finished the solitary meal, paid her check, and started out of the busy store. She hesitated at a cluster of paperback bookracks.

It was going to be an uneventful evening; might as well prepare for it with something interesting to read.

Donna made a project out of selecting her evening's entertainment. Her back to the row of open telephone cubicles that lined the back wall at Steuben's, she was deciding between a promisingly lively mystery and a bestseller dealing with the medical world when she became aware of a disturbingly familiar voice. Someone, using a public telephone just a few feet away, was saying, "Yeah, well, I still didn't like it. Yeah, well, make up your mind, you either go around with me or her!"

Donna half circled the bookrack, verifying her first impression; the caller was Tabby Lacer. It was not a surprising coincidence, considering that the drugstore was second only to Colton Park and the settlement-house area as a gang hangout.

Tabby sounded angry, which also was not surprising. "Listen, she's a dirty, double-crossing rat-fink. I told her we got this thing goin' Friday night – y'know, like we wanted her an' Jo-Jo to – y'know, with the baby buggy . . . like I said?"

Donna remained motionless, simultaneously puzzled and fascinated by the monologue. Tabby could have been talking about any one of her crowd, but intuition told

Donna the subject was Ann Julian. Seconds later, she learned that her hunch was right. Apparently Tabby was replying to some sort of protest from the other end of the line.

"Yeah, I gave 'er a hard time. Why shouldn't I? She's s'posed to be a Cat, ain't she? So why shouldn' she do a job when you guys got a rumble with the Steamers?"

There was an extended pause, during which Donna remained motionless, regretting her accidental role as an eavesdropper and wishing she could move away without attracting Tabby's attention. Tabby had turned to lean against a side partition of the enclosure. She went through an intricate one-handed maneuver of removing a cigarette from a crumpled pack and striking a match against a safety pack. Then, puffing furiously, and after several futile attempts to break into what was evidently a long, disturbing speech from the other party, Tabby growled, "Okay, but keep away from her. I'll see ya over by the show . . . yeah . . . 'bout a half hour. Uh-uh. What I said still goes, Chip. . . . Huh? What I said last *night*. . . . Sure, I meant it. . . ."

The earlier tirade, which had evidently revolved around Ann Julian, melted into what sounded like typical, unsophisticated girl-loves-boy talk; crude and obscure, but unquestionably sincere. Resentment and jealousy had given way to a warmer sentiment, and now Donna's embarrassment became acute. She lifted the detective story from the rack and hurried toward the check-out stand, fumbling in her handbag for change and keeping her head lowered to avoid Tabby's line of sight.

Donna released her breath as she stepped out of the store. Tabby hadn't seen her; an uncomfortable situation had been avoided.

She was inside her car, reaching to turn the ignition key when a chilling voice addressed her:

"I hope ya got an earful, stooge!"

Tabby folded her arms over the ledge of the open window, poking her face just inches away from Donna's. "What are ya, a cop or somethin', followin' me around?"

"I didn't! I mean . . ." Stupidly, knowing that her quick smile probably looked idiotic, Donna held up her purchase. "I stopped in to buy a book."

Tabby's expression remained unchanged. Her disbelief was emphasized by her tone. "Whatta ya know."

"Yes, I stopped to have dinner and then I . . ."

"Listen, what's *with* you, anyway?"

"Me?"

"Yeah, *you!* What's it to ya, what I do?"

95

Donna shifted to what she hoped was a careless attitude. "I couldn't possibly care less. What you do is your business."

"You sure took over Julian. You got her carryin' bedpans without even gettin' paid. Don't go messin' around too far, though. Know what I mean? Next thing I know, you start on Jo-Jo an' a couple other kids, lousin' everybody up."

Donna managed to explain that "lousin' everybody up" was certainly not in her plans. Tabby remained distrustful and arrogant. And her anger with Ann Julian seemed all out of proportion, if loyalty to the gang were her only concern. Her weight resting against the car, Tabby launched into a series of invectives, pouring out an almost pathological hatred for Ann. Amazing, Donna thought, especially since Ann had never been more than a minor member of Tabby's crowd. Donna risked saying as much. "I didn't think Ann was that important to you."

Tabby hesitated. The hard lines around her pale mouth tightened, and her heavily penciled eyes reflected a searing inner conflict. When she spoke again, the brassiness was gone from her tone, but the hatred was still there, strangely intensified in the subdued, throaty sound: "She don't mean a thing t' me."

"Then why should you care what Ann does?"

"I got my reasons," Tabby said.

Donna shrugged. "I suppose you have."

Tabby seemed dissatisfied with that casual dismissal. Quite obviously her war with Ann Julian was important to her; she wanted to talk about it. *"Personal* reasons," she emphasized.

Donna had an urge to ask if Chip O'Neill might have something to do with those "personal reasons." Common sense came to her rescue; she congratulated herself for putting down an impulse that could only have stirred up trouble. She was less successful in handling her second impulse: to prove to Tabby that hatred could bounce off some human beings and return to its sender in the form of friendship. The idea was accelerated by a driver who honked his horn and shouted, "You movin' out today, lady? I've been looking for a parking space for twenty minutes."

Donna started the motor. "Can I drop you anywhere? I'm going west on Colton, past the park."

Tabby appeared neither pleased nor surprised by the invitation. "You c'n gimme a lift t' the National," she said. She circled the car in a few agile steps, her stride long and

97

controlled, furthering the feline impression given by her name and by her catlike eyes. Seconds later she was seated beside Donna, puffing at the inevitable cigarette and filling the car with uncomfortable silence.

Donna concentrated, at first, on maneuvering a place in the jumbled stream of cars, trucks, and buses. When the quiet became too deadly, she made comments about the growing number of cars, the lack of parking areas, the weather. Her attempts at drawing Tabby into conversation were met with sullen quiet. Tabby might have lowered herself to accept a favor, but she was not about to break down the wall of animosity between herself and the rest of the world.

Donna made a project of trying to establish communication. As they wove through the traffic she gestured at a stalled car. "Poor devil!"

Tabby's response was an unsympathetic snort.

Donna commented on a police officer who was attempting to route a lane of traffic around the unfortunate driver. "I wouldn't want his job."

Tabby released a derogatory sound from between her teeth. *"Tchuh!"* It was a smug, superior sound, implying that only a fool would be concerned about a cop's problems.

As they drove past the park, Donna made another stab at establishing rapport. "This is such a pretty spot. It's wonderful for kids to have a place like this."

This time there was a muttered response. "Yeah. Crazy."

"I've always wanted to take up tennis. Do you ever come here to play tennis?"

Donna took her eye off the street long enough for a sidelong glance at Tabby's reaction. It revealed a contemptuous amusement.

"I come down here," Tabby said. "Yeah. I like t' play games."

"Tennis?" The question sounded ridiculous to Donna even as she asked it.

"Sort of. Swing somethin' around, see if y' can hit somethin'." Tabby seemed to enjoy the innuendo in her words.

Swing something. Hit something. Someone. Anyone. But strike out. Hit, hurt. Avenge the wrongs the world has inflicted upon you. Donna felt a tightening in her throat muscles. Not an hour ago she had been seized by a mounting fear as she crossed the parking lot opposite the settlement house. Whom had she feared? If she had been afraid of any specific person, that person must have been the girl seated next to her now.

But, at least, Tabby was responding now.

99

Bitterly, perhaps, but she was acknowledging Donna's existence. "I don't hang around the park too much. Just if there's some action."

"Action?"

Tabby blew a cloud of smoke at the windshield, obscuring Donna's view for a moment. "What'd ya wanna give me a ride fer? T' bust your jaw askin' a lotta questions?"

It was impossible to talk with the girl. Gar had been right; it was like beating your head against a stone wall. To show sympathy meant to invite contempt. To show interest meant aggravating an innate suspicion.

Donna gave up. They passed the park, crossing the street on which Donna lived. Again the silence became oppressive, and it seemed natural to say, "That's where I live. That graystone apartment building there."

"Too bad for you," Tabby responded.

"Too bad . . .?"

Tabby didn't explain, and Donna concluded that the remark was a facetious one; "too bad" for anyone who lived in a decent place. What did they want – Tabby's pity? "My heart bleeds for you, you've got it so rough." This, in essence, was what Tabby was saying.

Donna shifted the conversational gear once more. "The National. That's over on Vesper Street, isn't it? Vesper and Thirty-fifth?"

"Yeah. Six more blocks. So I'll get off here."

"No, I'll . . ."

"You live in this block? So who needs you to go six more blocks? Lemme off on the next corner. *Dig?*"

"Really, it's no trouble. I've had dinner, and I don't have any plans for the . . ."

"Lemme off on the next corner," Tabby hissed.

Donna obliged. She might as well have been talking in Urdu, for all the contact that had been made. She was not thanked for the small favor. Moreover, there was a disconcerting awareness that while Tabby resented any kindness that might be shown to her, she simultaneously prided herself in having played you for a sucker if you were barely civil to her!

Tabby got out of the car without looking directly at Donna, staring down the street in either real or feigned concentration, establishing that her destination was of more interest to her. "See ya aroun'," she muttered.

Donna waved, but she said nothing. Why encourage the girl's rudeness, or indicate approval of that callous front? Real or affected, Tabby's indifference certainly didn't merit approval. And if this was what it meant to deal with a hard-core case, it wasn't worth the effort.

Later, when she was alone, Donna's attitude softened again. She tried to see Tabby Lacer in the light of her conditioning; forced herself to regard the hard-as-nails toughness and cheap appearance as natural by-products of Tabby's childhood. It was difficult. It had been more gratifying to extend a friendly hand to Ann Julian, to have the friendship gratefully returned and richly rewarded. Tabby, if there was hope for her at all, was not a case for what Gar called amateur do-gooders. She was a problem to which the professional psychologists, sociologists, and juvenile officers were welcome.

Still later, Donna began to have qualms about the entire situation and especially her part in it. She had learned that Tabby was virtually unreachable. She had learned that some real or imagined grievance had aimed Tabby's anger directly at Ann Julian. If it was jealousy that was eating at Tabby, the results could be disastrous.

For wasn't jealousy the most painful of all torments? So devastating that even a mild-mannered and well-adjusted pediatrics nurse could spend a sleepless night wracked by that pain for which there is no cure?

TEN

The "tomorrow" Gar had questioned, and about which Donna worried, passed uneventfully. So did the next day, and the next.

If there was any notice taken of gang activity in the East Colton Street district, it was a story in the evening edition of the *Times*. Tipped off about an impending teenage gang fight between the Colton Conquests and the Steamers, extra policemen had been assigned to Colton Park on Friday night. The presence of the officers had averted the proposed rumble. Peace reigned in the settlement-house area.

Ann Julian was presented with a violet cologne and bath powder set by the grateful patients of a ward at the County Hospital, a gift for "services over and above the call of duty"; Ann made a special trip to the clinic to show her treasured award to Donna. If this was the jungle, then the tigers slumbered quietly, and peace blessed the lesser animals.

One afternoon, several days after reading about the aborted gang battle, Donna greeted a totally unexpected visitor, one who walked into the pediatrics clinic's reception room with an awareness that he was completely out of place.

Donna smiled at the boy, partly in an effort to put him at ease, but mostly because the hulking, yellow-haired teen-ager looked so completely bewildered by his surroundings. "Hello. Is there something I can do for you?"

"Maybe," he replied. "Yeah, maybe you could."

He wore the wavy blond hair in a fashion currently popular with local hoods: long, grotesquely parted in two places, curling into wide sideburns and back to a modified version of what was once known as a ducktail. He had an unusually handsome and arrogant face; square-jawed and, ironically, enhanced by a nose that showed signs of having once been broken. Worn blue jeans and a black leather jacket (the latter incongruous, considering the warm weather) completed the tough-guy illusion. The only conflicting note in the junior-grade hoodlum picture he presented were his eyes. Deep set, wide, bluer than Gar Breverman's, the boy's eyes made a mockery of all the external effects with which he had adorned himself. They made him look, Donna thought, like somebody's extremely likable and frightened kid brother.

He sauntered over to Donna's desk,

affecting the same bored and sneering attitude that she had observed in Tabby Lacer. The difference was that Tabby made the pose come off; the boy would have looked more natural on a bicycle, waving a cheerful hello to a paper-route customer. "You Donna Marker?" he asked.

She almost laughed at the gutteral monosyllables. She wanted to say, "Yes, me Donna. You Tarzan?" but she restrained herself. "That's right. Can I help you?"

"I was wonderin'," the boy said. "You seen Ann yet?"

"Ann Julian?"

"Yeah. She been around?"

Donna checked her watch. "N-no. She doesn't always stop in, especially on days when we're really busy here. She'd have been here by now if she had planned to see me."

"You didn't see her today?"

Something of the boy's alarm transferred itself to Donna. "No. She's probably picked up Timmy by now and gone home. Her brother stays at . . ."

"I know all that," the boy interrupted. His face, extremely youthful and almost baby-faced in spite of the rugged jawline, had clouded over with concern.

"Are you a friend of Ann's?" Donna asked.

"Maybe I am," the boy said. Somehow, the

105

belligerent sentence fell flat. He seemed to sense that, and he covered up by adding, "I had a date to meet her. Outside school."

"Her high school?"

"Yeah. I was late, though. I got loused up an' I didn't get there when I said I would."

"You don't go to Ann's school, then?"

"Nah, I quit."

"That's too bad."

"Huh?"

"I said it's too bad you quit."

"Yeah. Well, don't cry any big tears about it." The boy edged toward the door. "Listen, I gotta cut. If Ann comes in here . . . ."

"I'll tell her Chip O'Neill was looking for her," Donna said.

Her impulsive guess had been correct; Chip did an astounded double take. "Hey, how'd you know . . . did Ann tell you about me?"

Donna resisted another of the innumerable impulses that plagued her; the temptation to say, "No, but Tabby did. Indirectly." Instead, she told Chip the white lie he evidently hoped to hear. "Yes, Ann's mentioned your name."

"I'll cruise on by her house," Chip said.

"That's the thing to do," Donna agreed. "If she's already picked up Timmy."

"That's what's buggin' me," Chip said. He

was at the door. "The kid's still here. She wouldn't of gone home without him."

Donna rose from her seat behind the desk. "Are you sure she wasn't delayed at school?"

"I asked around. A couple of kids saw her leave. So I went the way I figured she'd go, but I didn't see her. Maybe" – Chip's forehead tortured itself into a row of furrows – "I dunno. Maybe she took some kind of a short-cut. She shoulda been here, though. By *this* time."

He remembered to say, "Thanks a lot," as he left the clinic. And he left behind him a distinct impression of being worried about Ann, and with good cause.

Chip O'Neill's concern was not a product of his imagination.

Shortly after four o-clock, Donna returned a wailing infant to its mother's arms. She assured the woman that having a baby immunized against diphtheria, whooping cough, and tetanus would more than compensate for tears resulting from a quick needle pinch. The woman beamed, and Donna checked to see who had come into the reception room.

It was Gar Breverman, and his usual easy grin was conspicuously missing from his face. "Donna . . . I hope you're not too busy."

"Why? What's wrong?"

"Ann Julian. A couple of youngsters found her in an alley near the high school."

Donna gasped for breath. "She's not . . ."

"She'll be all right," Gar assured her. "But she's had a rough go of it. Someone beat her up. Black eyes, lacerations. The doc told me it's a miracle she didn't have any ribs broken, or internal injuries. Whoever did it wasn't playing games. She was kicked and beaten senseless."

For a moment the room threatened to collapse, spinning around Donna sense lessly, closing in on her. She heard herself whispering, "Oh no. My God, no!"

And then Gar was telling Dr. Janis that Donna would be back soon, that he wanted to take her across the street to County. Gar was arranging everything and guiding Donna to a ward in which Ann lay still as death, her delicate face horribly bruised. She was conscious, though her lips were purple and hideously swollen.

Donna leaned over the hospital bed. "Ann! Oh, Annie, I'm so sorry! We should have watched out for you!"

Ann Julian's eyes filled with tears. Gar had left the room, but she tried to lift her head, looking around to make sure that she was alone with Donna. Satisfied, Ann whispered,

"It's not your fault. I . . . told you that . . . the other day."

"Who did this to you, Ann? Dr. Breverman said you won't tell anyone."

"I don't know."

"Didn't you see who did it?"

"No!" Ann's shrill protest must have sounded weak even to her own ears. She made a desperate attempt to be convincing. "I didn't see them. It just . . . *happened*."

Any nurse would have known better than to pursue the subject. Ann had suffered a terrible shock; arguing with her would only prove upsetting. "All right," Donna said quietly. "You didn't see who dragged you into that alley. I'll have to take your word for it. But . . . if you should remember, honey, please tell the police. You won't have to be afraid of anyone. Maybe the gang believed in getting its own revenge without calling on the law. You're not a gang member anymore. You're a law-abiding citizen, and the officers are on your side. They want to protect you, see that whoever hurt you doesn't do it again."

Donna spoke as though she were talking to Ann's little brother – simply, patiently – spelling out the elementary concepts in terms that any child could understand. It was a losing battle. Ann Julian remained adamant; either she didn't know the identity of her assailants (she had implied that there were several), or fear of further retribution had paralyzed her, sealing her to the "no cops" code of the underworld – even that puny juvenile underworld led by Tabby Lacer.

But though she wouldn't name her attackers, Ann seemed anxious to explain why she had been assaulted. "See . . . Chip never paid any attention to me before. He was sort of . . . you know, hands off. Tabby's private property. He wouldn't have noticed me anyway. He's too big a wheel in the neighborhood."

"He must have noticed you somewhere along the line," Donna encouraged. "He came to the clinic looking for you today. I think he was the one who started the search for you, when he didn't find you at home and you didn't show up at the nursery."

"He's been meeting me after school every day. He comes to our place . . . like, if I'm not on duty at the hospital" – Ann closed her eyes for a moment and sighed – "he comes over and we talk. He's really neat."

A school drop-out, Donna recalled. Leader of a gang called the Colton Conquests. Tabby Lacer served as his chain and broken-bottle bearer when his gang engaged in one of those vicious and senseless outbursts of violence minimizingly called a rumble. Yet Ann was

110

saying he was really neat. And a few hours ago, Donna, too, had been thinking that Chip O'Neill was totally unsuited for his role as a juvenile thug.

"He's been coming to see you, then?"

Ann was having trouble speaking, but she seemed anxious to go on. "Uh-huh. First thing he noticed . . . how different I look. Y'know, with my hair cut, and the cute uniform. He saw me coming home from the hospital one night. I about died, he was so nice to me . . . said all these neat things. Then I asked him over to meet my mom and watch TV. He couldn't get over our place. I mean, he expected it to look real dumpy, like the rest of the building . . . like the place where he lives, a couple of blocks down. He couldn't get over how pretty everything looks. It really does, too. I keep it just the way you helped me fix it up."

Donna patted Ann's hand. It was difficult to hold back tears, seeing the girl's pride in a rundown tenement flat to which a scrub brush and a few cheap decorating touches had lent a bit of magic.

"Chip's dad is a cab driver. He has all these brothers and sisters. His mom died a couple years ago, and I guess where he lives . . . it must be a real mess the way he talks about it. His dad's like my mom used to be . . . all beat out, so he doesn't pay any attention to the kids. I told Chip he ought to take over, instead of runnin' around and trying to be a big shot."

"What does he say to that?"

"Oh, it's rough. He'd sort of like to be a draftsman. That's what he told me one night. He used to get real good grades in drafting. Before he quit school. I told him he oughta go back. Graduate. Then he could get a good job and move out of this crumby neighborhood."

"I didn't think gang leaders were interested in good jobs," Donna said.

"He acts like he's not. Sometimes. It all depends. If he's talking to me, Chip's ... well, he's really *himself*. He sees me working at the hospital and planning how I'm going to go into nurse's training and all. Well, like he says, *that* takes guts. Doing it ... sort of the *hard* way. You can't be chicken and do something that's really hard for you to do. Y'see?"

Donna nodded. "I certainly do. With all the strikes against Chip, if *he* got somewhere in the world, nobody could call him chicken."

"I know. I keep telling him that, and he digs it, too. But there's –" Ann paused, searching for words to explain a sociological problem that stumped people whose knowledge far exceeded hers, "there's the way you're brought up if you live around here. You're nobody if you let anybody push you around. Maybe you don't even want to fight ... like Chip didn't want to fight at the park the other night. He couldn't call it off. See, all the guys would have thought he was ..."

"Chicken," Donna said. There seemed to be only one word, only one criterion of status in the juvenile jungle. "He didn't want his gang to think he was chicken."

"Sure. So here I am, I'm telling him what's the *sense* of it Chip? You beat up some guys, or they beat you up. What's the *sense?* Maybe one guy gets hurt real bad – *dies*, even. Then you go to jail. Big deal! You get cooped up and have to take orders from people.... It's not like *being* somebody and having your own money, and nobody can get tough with you or tell you what to do because it's really *yours*. You earned it because you know how to do something better than anyone else. Say, I'm a nurse, and Chip goes in for drafting. We could even live in a nice house and have friends and everything. We'd never have to be scared of anybody! There's places like that. Everybody just works and has fun and fixes up their own place. You know ... like you see in the movies."

Donna nodded sagely. To Ann, a decent

home, a respectable job, and not having to trample down someone else to keep from being trampled . . . all this was a movieland dream! Yet, unlike most of the East Colton Street area inhabitants, she had begun to see the dream as a not-impossible reality for herself. Beaten black and blue, but evangelizing – selling the happy dream to the leader of the Colton Conquests! "I've made some mistakes," Donna thought. "I may be responsible for that pitifully swollen face. But I opened a door for Ann, and I'm proud of it."

Ann seemed determined to finish her expiation of Chip. "Lots of times he'd be . . . well, he wouldn't be doing much of anything, but he wouldn't be getting into trouble, either. And Tabby . . . she'd sort of shove him into something. Dare him to take on some other gang. Then he'd do it, just to prove he was a big operator."

"Like what?"

"Oh . . . steal stuff. Rough up somebody. Challenge the Rippers or the Tenth-Street Knights. Stuff like that. She used to be his chick. His . . . girlfriend."

"Used to be?" Donna was remembering Tabby's date to meet Chip in front of the National Theater.

"It wasn't serious with him. It just sort of happened – like, both of them were at

114

the top and who else could they go with?"
A sweet half-smile softened Ann's bruised
features. "He likes me, though. He likes me
a lot, Donna."

"And you?"

"I guess –" Ann had been given a sedative,
but the dreamy quality of her voice had not
been induced by drugs, "I guess I . . . just
about love Chip better than anybody in the
whole world."

It was all clear then. Tabby Lacer's phone
call, her jealousy, the savage beating, Chip's
worried visit to the clinic this afternoon. All
clear and painfully obvious.

Nothing remained but waiting to see what
Tabby would do next.

ELEVEN

Donna returned to a madhouse of bawling
babies and impatient mothers; her forty-five
minute absence from the clinic had been
enough to blow Dr. Janis's schedule to
smithereens.

It was close to six o'clock before hectic
teamwork had cleared the reception room
of the last tiny patient. Only one advantage

resulted from this concentration of work: Donna had no time to brood over Ann's misfortune or her own responsibility for what had happened.

"Pam's going to have a fit," Walter Janis said when he and Donna were finally alone. "We were going to have dinner early and try to see the Home Show. It's way across town, and it'll be a race to get her back here by eleven." He looked ruefully at the disorder left behind during the examining-room rush. "I hate to ask you to stay any later than this."

"Well, we're not going to open the doors on *this* tomorrow," Donna told him. "Schedule's jammed until four o'clock tomorrow. You go get Pammy. . . . She's been talking about that Home Show all week."

"Really?"

Donna had started the process of cleaning up the debris. "Of course! All women are interested in having a nice home someday. You should have heard Ann Julian this afternoon!"

Dr. Janis was usually interested in what he called "Donna's Ann Project," but this time, in spite of his hurry, he refused to let the conversation shift away from Pam Hollis. "Talks about a home of her own, eh? Pam?"

"Sure."

"Hm."

116

"Is that so strange?"

The doctor slipped into his suit jacket. "She started off giving me the impression that she likes the bachelor-girl life. Yesterday she said she wanted to see this show to . . . to get ideas for fixing up your apartment."

Donna picked up two tongue depressors that had missed the wastebasket. "I hate to tell tales out of school. But if you're pumping me for information" – she looked up at the doctor's eager expression and laughed – "and I think you *are* . . ."

"All right, all right, I want to know if she's thinking Domestic Suburbia."

"She's thinking Domestic Suburbia, Doc. When she's not wondering what you're thinking."

"Maybe I should tell her," he said, as though the thought had just occurred to him. "Maybe I should tell her tonight."

"Don't say I pushed you into a serious lifelong step."

"I will, too, say it! Oh, look, let this go. . . . The janitor will get everything else, and we'll get at the instruments first thing in . . ."

"Good night!" Donna said. He was out of the room in a matter of seconds, calling back apologies for rushing off, and cautioning Donna not to stay too late. She heard him whistling as he walked toward the parking lot

117

across the street, a tuneless, off-key whistle that made up for its sour notes by filling the air with buoyant enthusiasm.

There was something satisfying about doing physical work when your nerves were on edge. Donna plunged into the straightening process, completed it, and still felt a need to spend her energy. The patient file had needed reorganizing for a long time; having dinner alone seemed less appealing than getting the files in order. After that, there were two cartons of literature from the County Health Department to open, stacks of brochures on infant care and immunization to place where young mothers would be sure to see them.

There were other distractions after that. Donna found herself working compulsively, wondering from time to time if the offices next door were still occupied. Once, overcome more by hope than by curiosity, she stepped outside the door to see if Gar's convertible was still parked across the way. It was not. There were no signs of activity in the office next door. Someone crossed the parking lot, but she was unable to make out the shadowy figure, and the fleeting, wishful thought that Gar might be returning for evening sessions in his office collapsed. It was replaced by depressing conjectures about where he might be at this hour ... and with whom. Work was the only escape hatch from the gloomy dungeon of aloneness; Donna cleaned out a supply cabinet that needed her attention considerably less than she needed diversion.

Hunger pangs finally ended the manic process. Donna washed her hands, ran a desultory comb through her hair and daubed on fresh lipstick, though she was too tired to do any more than drive the short distance home, and it was doubtful that anyone would see her between the office and the refrigerator she intended to raid at home.

It wasn't until she was ready to leave that Donna realized that it didn't get dark out until after eight, and that she'd had the lights on for at least an hour. Checking her watch revealed that it was past nine o'clock; the county had been more than repaid for the time off she had taken this afternoon. If the health department really wanted its money's worth, she thought, it should concentrate on hiring nurses who were hopelessly in love with men who didn't return the compliment.

There was a second reaction to the time, following that bitterly amusing thought. As Donna locked the door behind her, there was an automatic acceleration of her heartbeat. She glanced along the long wall of the building. There were no lights burning; the settlement house was dark and vacant. A

119

glaring white street light cast long shadows across the parking lot: grotesquely distorted telephone poles and the outlines of a brick enclosing wall. There was only one car visible, her own, parked against the farthest end of the wall. Donna drew a deep breath and started walking toward it, seeing the automobile as a haven of safety, sanctuary.

She started walking swiftly, looking straight ahead. Unconsciously she speeded her pace. And then she was running, her flesh suddenly cold and clammy against her nylon uniform. Running, keeping her eyes fixed on the goal, and reminding herself silently that the sounds she heard behind her were imaginary; noises conjured up out of fear, out of regret for the stupid delay in leaving the building until there was no one around. No one to hear her cries if someone, something . . .

The sounds were real. Panic-stricken, Donna caught a frightened breath. The audible whimpering sound solidified her fear. Without looking backward, she speeded up her race across the vast dirt area, straining every muscle in a frantic attempt to escape someone who was running after her – and gaining.

Her car was only a few yards away. With a super-human effort she might reach it. Donna thrust herself forward, and in almost the same

120

instant saw the figure rise from where it had apparently been crouching during the chase; an imposing black silhouette that materialized like a nightmare apparition from behind the hood of the car. Even in the uncertain light, the exaggerated balloon of straw-yellow hair identified Tabby Lacer.

Donna stopped short, feeling as though someone had jabbed a knife under her ribs.

Heavy footsteps and the sounds of panting breath closed in from behind Donna. There had been two of them following her; they came into sight now, closing a tight ring around her. Jo-Jo and Nicki. Tabby and her top-echelon Cats, ominous and unmistakably hostile. A fearful cry froze in Donna's throat; her body seemed to have turned to ice.

"You in a hurry or somethin'?" Tabby purred.

Jo-Jo guffawed.

"I guess," Nicki said. She was out of breath, but the words were hissed from between her teeth.

Tabby advanced a step forward. "Goin' somewhere?" She towered over Donna, her arrogance cool and measured. Her flunkies tightened the ring by edging closer to their quarry.

Donna forced herself to stand erect, to keep her voice from wavering. "I'm going home."

"Hear that? She's goin' *straight home!*"

There was the usual appreciative response to Tabby's insinuating remark.

"I don't know what you want from me, Tabby. If it's a lift, you're welcome. If you're looking for trouble, you're liable to find more than you can handle."

Tabby pushed her chalky face forward. The bizarre underscoring of her eyes gave the effect of a Halloween mask. "You think you can handle some, Nursie?" Jo-Jo and Nicki moved in closer.

It was hard to keep from screaming for help. Or perhaps it was impossible to cry out. Every nerve in Donna's system seemed to be drawn taut, almost beyond its tensile strength. "How many of you did it take to . . . handle Ann this afternoon? She's tiny. Maybe only two of you."

"Ann? Did somebody do something to Ann?" Tabby pursed her lips in mock surprise.

"Wouldn't that be a shame," Jo-Jo said.

Nicki lifted a corner of her mouth. "Yeah, ain't it terrible what happens to some people."

"Especially when they go blabbin' too much," Tabby said. "Like nosin' in on private phone conversations an' then squealin' it all to the fuzz."

Donna opened her mouth to protest.

122

"Don't try wigglin' out of it, ya scuzzy rat-fink! How could the cops know there was a big blast on last Friday? They wouldn't find it out from nobody except you, 'cause you heard me talkin' about it."

"That's not . . ."

"Okay, so maybe you foun' out from Julian. An' I'll tell ya how I feel about Julian!"

"*Yeah*," Jo-Jo emphasized. "Let's tell 'er how."

"I gotta better idea," Nicki muttered. "How 'bout we *show* 'er?"

They wouldn't dare. They'd be afraid to attack someone who could identify them later, Donna thought. The desperate reasoning failed to take Ann into account. They might assume that fear of reprisal would keep Donna quiet. Or they might not think at all, as savage animals don't think. Or . . . they might be sadistic enough not to have to worry about being identified because they would be thorough. . . .

Reason with them? Appeal to conscience? Plead with the kind of scum that stomped cripples and old people for a handful of change, ganged up on terrified school-children in the park, sometimes for pennies and sometimes just for the pleasure of demonstrating their power?

Donna tensed her body, waiting for the
123

onslaught. Jo-Jo stepped behind her. The sullen red-haired girl took a step backward, too.

"They're going to try to pin back my arms," Donna thought. Her glance swept quickly from Tabby's hideously long fingernails to the far end of the lot, her mind exploring a possible avenue of escape. Make a break now? Run, screaming, for the street, in the hope that a car might be passing? How far would she get? Break away *now*?

She stood paralyzed, convinced now that the hopeless odds would paralyze her further still, so that she would not be able to fight back or even protect herself from this nightmare of barbarism.

Frantic thoughts, crowding over each other during a momentary silence that probably lasted no more than a few seconds, but was made seemingly endless by the fearful suspense. Then Tabby's menacing voice: "I'd like t' know why we're wastin' all this time!" And, in almost the same instant, the sweeping flash of lights and Jo-Jo's alarmed cry. "Hey . . . the cops!"

Tabby whirled out of the light beam, ordering, "Let's cut!"

Automobile headlights blinded Donna, then swerved as the car advanced. Twin spotlights caught the Tabby Cat trio rounding the corner and disappearing behind the parking lot wall.

Donna covered her face with her hands, leaning against the door of her own car for support. Her legs trembled, threatening to buckle under her.

As the squad car ground to a stop at her side, a male voice shouted, "Are you all right, miss?"

Another male voice, this one arrestingly familiar, repeated the question with a more personal concern. "Donna, are you all right?"

She nodded weakly, uncovering her face in time to see Gar Breverman open the back door of the police car and get out.

"We'll swing back for you," one of the officers said.

"Right." Gar slammed the door and the black sedan roared toward the alley, leaving a dark plume of dust behind it.

Gar closed the distance between himself and Donna in three quick strides. "Donna, are you sure they . . . ? Here, let me see you."

He might have been the father of a disobedient injured child, examining her with mingled compassion and sternness. "Do you realize what could have happened to you out here at this hour?"

She began to cry then, releasing the pent-up fear and sudden relief in convulsive sobs that shuddered through her body. And Gar was no longer lecturing her; he was holding her fast in his arms, kissing her forehead, then brushing her tears aside with his lips and murmuring over and over again, "It's all right now. Don't cry, Donna ... you're all right ... nothing's going to happen to you. ..."

Donna clung to him, her eyes pressed shut, fiercely grateful for the miracle of his warmth, for the unbelievable security of his strong arms encircling her. She felt like a sleeper awakened from a terrifying ordeal and finding the sweet escape more unreal than the nightmare.

She was calmer when Gar walked her to her car. He sat beside her while they waited for the police car to return, and though her hysteria was under control and there was no justification for his holding her hand, Gar held it anyway.

"I kept cruising past your office all evening," he said. "In my own car, Martinez and Gavin were looking for a couple of the Tabby girls ... wanted to question them about what happened to Ann this afternoon. We seemed to be covering the same route, so I joined them."

"The police?"

"Yes. We work together closely on some cases, the way our clinic cooperates with the probation department, for example."

"Gar?"

"Mm?"

"I know all that. You . . . said something else, though. You were driving past the clinic all evening. Why?"

Gar looked faintly embarrassed for a moment. After an uncomfortable pause, he said, "I knew you were working late. I saw your car out here when I left my office, and I knew Dr. Janis had gone home. I stopped to have dinner, but I couldn't stop worrying about you. So . . ." Gar lifted his hands in a gesture of helpless resignation. "What could I do? I tried to keep an eye on you. Must have missed you by just a fraction. . . . We drove by here no more than two or three minutes ago."

They were silent while Donna pondered what he had said; perhaps Gar was weighing the same thoughts. Why would he spend his entire evening patroling the parking lot area if he was as indifferent as he had indicated? A man could be protective without kissing your forehead repeatedly; he could console you without holding you as though you might disintegrate if he let you go.

Officers Martinez and Gavin returned to the parking lot within ten minutes, and without Tabby, Nicki, and Jo-Jo. They knew where

127

they could find the trio, the officers reported. But they could not pick them up unless a complaint was filed. Did Miss Marker wish to press charges against the girls?

Terrifying as her experience had been, Donna was forced to come to an honest conclusion. She had not been injured. Except by implication (and imagination!), she had not even been threatened. Had she seen any signs of a weapon? A switchblade knife, a club or gun? Nothing except Tabby's long, garishly painted fingernails. No one had laid a hand on her, and if she had been pursued, it was only because she had chosen to run. The gang's intentions had been clear, of course. But they could not be hauled into the police station because you *thought* they were going to beat you senseless.

"No charges," Donna said.

Gar shook his head, disgusted. "Every time they get away with something like this, we take a long step backward."

"We're going to round them up, anyway," Officer Gavin said. "Strictly for conversation about the Julian case." A huge, florid-faced young man, he spoke in the disparaging tone of one who knows his efforts will be futile. "The Julian girl either didn't see who pulled her into that alley, or else she's clammed up out of fear. If there were any witnesses,

128

they're playing it safe by being quiet. All we can do is play a hunch and ask a few questions. Want us to drive you over to your car, Doc? We'll follow Miss Marker home."

"No, thanks," Gar said. "We'll manage."

Donna thanked them, too. And as the squad car sped off the lot once more, she learned what Gar meant by "We'll manage."

"My car's just around the corner, in front of the gym. Let's go get it, and I'll follow you home. If you aren't too shook up to drive, that is."

"You've gone to a lot of trouble already," Donna told him. "I'm sure I'd be safe . . . just driving home a few blocks."

"Am I being dismissed?"

"Oh no. No, I . . . hate to impose upon you any more, that's all."

"Impose upon me," Gar said firmly

Donna started the motor. "You must think I'm an awful ninny."

"I do. Which doesn't do anything except prove that you need me around." He must have realized at once that the words made him sound egotistical and officious. In the next breath, Gar ridiculed his role as her strong protector. "Notice the timing? All heroes have excellent timing. We appear at the crucial moment, charging in on our white

129

horses, rescuing the helpless maiden from evil forces."

"It wasn't funny," Donna reminded him. "I'm still shaking . . . inside *and* out."

Gar agreed soberly. "No, it wasn't funny. Funny it was not. I was only ridiculing my part in it. You know, I didn't have to act like a lovesick schoolboy, walking past his girlfriend's house all evening long. An *adult* would have knocked on your office door."

"I . . ." Donna paused.

"You what?"

"I had sort of . . . hoped that you might."

It was a short drive to the spot where Gar's convertible was parked. They drove it in silence, again retiring to separate chambers of thought. When Donna had parked her car at the curb, Gar opened the door at his side. "I missed my dinner," he said. "Doesn't that stir some sense of obligation in you?"

"Well, if you're going to convoy me home I suppose I should invite you up."

Gar smiled. "You impose on me, I'll impose on you. Shall we stop at a take-out place and pick up something? Ribs? Chicken?"

"What's wrong with leftover Irish stew?"

"I'll tell you after I've tried it. Pass me up, and don't drive too fast. I don't want you out of my sight."

He had started to walk toward the Buick

when Donna called, "Gar?"

He turned back. "Something wrong?"

"Nothing's wrong. I was just thinking. You're spending a whole lifetime, making a career of figuring out what makes people tick."

"So?"

"So . . . who figures out what makes *you* tick?"

He laughed aloud and climbed into the convertible, waiting for Donna to precede him, then trailing her down the gloomy street and into the Colton Street thoroughfare. She could glance into her rearview mirror and see him keeping his promise not to let her out of sight.

Insane to think of it this way. But as frightening as Donna's encounter with the Tabby Cats had been, she would always remember it with some degree of gratitude.

TWELVE

Donna barely tasted the food. She was relieved to notice that Gar wolfed down two portions and solemnly swore that his own mother had never made better stew.

131

"You'd better tell that to Pam Hollis," Donna said. "She made it, I didn't."

Gar scowled. "I wasted all that flattery? At least tell me you made the peach pie."

"Frozen," she said. "Packaged. I'm sorry."

Gar shrugged and started to help clear off the dinette table. "The coffee was good. I *saw* you make that."

Donna surveyed the remains of their late dinner. "Let's let all this go. I've had quite a day."

Gar agreed. "So you have. So you have. Your little project gal's doing all right, though."

"Fine." Donna had phoned the hospital twice during the evening, once from her desk and once while the warmed-over dinner was bubbling on the stove. "She's asleep . . . amazingly calm, considering what she's just gone through."

"You're doing rather well yourself. I get cold chills when I think what might have happened."

"Might and did are two different stories." Donna moved toward the living room.

"Ann wasn't lucky enough to have a knight in shining armor handy."

"Sir Lancelot will be happy to rinse these dishes for you. I know you're exhausted."

"They'll wait."

132

"I'm a very methodical guy."

Donna seated herself on the Danish sofa. "I know. You're proper, thorough, sensible. You look before you leap, and you never overlook a detail." She sighed. "I have enough of that on duty. Off duty, I like to follow my impulses."

Gar sank down beside her. "Following impulses can get you into trouble."

"I know."

"Following impulses, you can risk getting your silly head bashed in. You can also set someone else's carefully planned program back at least one year."

"Did I do that?" Donna asked.

Gar lifted her chin with his index finger. "You're a busybody and a scatterbrain. Sometimes I think you don't have the sense you were born with. And then again . . ." His voice dropped to a harsh whisper. "Then I realize it's not your head that's soft. It's your heart. No brains, all heart. You want to know something else, dimwit?"

Donna could only stare, tremulous, conscious of nothing but the magnetism emanating from him.

I love you.

It was too much. In another minute she would begin to cry again. "I told you I've had

. . . quite a day. I'm not sure I can . . . absorb any more."

"Sure you can." Gar pulled her into his arms. "That's the one more thing we can always take on, Donna. Somebody loves us." He kissed her, a long, revealing kiss, as hungry as her own response. "Tell *me*," he said quietly. "Same old words. Tell me, Donna."

"I love you."

He pressed her closer to him. "And do you know, darling . . . I didn't realize it until *tonight?* When I saw that crowd of she-coyotes around your car, and I had no way of knowing if . . ." Gar interrupted himself to cover Donna's face with kisses. "In the time it took for Martinez to drive across that lot, I died a thousand deaths. Up until then, I thought I was looking out for you out of . . . responsibility. Because I'd goaded you into getting involved over your head."

"Dimwit," Donna said.

"Brainless nincompoop, impulsive idiot. I didn't think I was capable of loving anyone the way I love you."

Terrible, world-shaking Paradise, Donna thought. The devastating sensation of having all your dreams suddenly come true. As though it weren't awesome enough to be this much in love – to suddenly discover that your love was returned! She buried her head against Gar's chest. "Do you know what I'm going to do, Gar?"

"Cry?"

"Mm-hm."

"That's logical," Gar said. "It's psychologically sound. Feel free to use either shoulder, honey."

He drew her into what was probably a psychologically sound shoulder-crying position, patting her hair with his hand and releasing a deep, satisfied sigh.

It was like being disturbed by cannon fire to hear the front door open. Donna leaped from the sofa; Gar sat up, startled.

"Donna?" Pam swept into the living room, strangely breathless, and a far cry from her usually cool, composed self. "Oh, I'm so glad you're home!"

Walter Janis followed Pam into the room; he was beaming, too. Both of them noticed Gar at the same time, greeting him with exceptionally warm enthusiasm as he rose to his feet.

"I thought you were going to the Home Show," Donna said. She hoped her disappointment wasn't too obvious.

"We had a brief look at it," Dr. Janis said. He grinned at Pam, looking for all the world like a five-year-old caught with jam

135

on his face.

We were in a hurry to get back here," Pam explained. "We . . ." She looked toward Walter for support.

"We want you to be the first to know," the doctor finished.

"Don't tell me . . ."

Pam broke into Donna's question, dropping her usual reserve completely and hugging her roommate. "We're going to get married. Walter's asked me . . . we're getting married next month."

There were exuberant congratulations from Donna and Gar, and delighted, self-conscious "thank-you" remarks from the happy couple. The engagement was toasted, for lack of champagne, in ginger ale. And it was not until the party atmosphere had begun to wear off, not until Pam had expressed her hope that Donna would be able to find someone suitable to share the apartment and Gar had muttered, "Oh, she'll manage to find some-one" – it was not until then that Walter Janis said, "We've been monopolizing the situa-tion, Pammy. We haven't even asked about Donna's day. Have you phoned the hospital, Donna?"

"Yes. Ann's doing very well."

Pam made a clucking sound with her tongue. "Poor kid. I remember how critical I was, the time she came here. I actually warned Donna not to get involved. And I've had to eat my words."

Gar raised an inquiring brow; he had been twice as critical as Pam. "She's done well at the hospital, I hear."

"In Surgery, especially on the night shift, we aren't too aware of Candy Stripers. But that girl's established a reputation. Even the doctors know her by name . . . talking about what a boost she's been for patient morale."

"And you know what cold fish doctors are," Walter Janis said archly.

Pam pressed her hand into his. "Let's just say they're sometimes slow to notice things."

It was beginning to get downright sticky, Donna thought. Perhaps Pam and Walter were as anxious to be alone with each other as she was to be alone with Gar. And Gar was beginning to fidget, looking at his watch from time to time, and adding almost nothing to the conversation. It was for this reason that Donna decided not to prolong the conversation when Pam said, "So Ann's coming along all right. Good. Anything else happen today?"

"Not a thing," Donna replied. Her eyes met Gar's for an instant. He was shaking his head in that slow, incredulous way of his, but this time his disbelief was warm with affection.

"Donna had an extremely uneventful evening," Gar said. "Humdrum, dull and ordinary."

It hadn't been any of those things, but why take the edge off Pam's announcement by describing a harrowing experience with a trio of barely civilized kids? "Until Gar came along," Donna modified. She might almost have been talking about all of her life before this evening. "It *was*. By comparison, humdrum, dull and ordinary."

THIRTEEN

In the days that followed, Donna no longer observed the fruits of her project alone. Gar was at her side when she drove Ann Julian home from the hospital. He sat in the Julians' flat and nodded approvingly while Mrs. Julian talked about the radical changes Donna had brought into her life and the lives of her children.

"She's passing it on, too," Ann's mother said proudly. "She's talking about getting us out of this neighborhood, even sending

Timmy to college someday."

Gar smiled. "That's a long way off."

"Oh, she's looking *way* ahead," Mrs. Julian fixed a proud smile on her daughter. "I'm still worried about her, with those gang girls running around loose and Ann walking . . ."

"I told you, you don't have to worry," Ann broke in. Her face still showed faint signs of the blue marks that had been inflicted by "unknown assailants," but she moved around the small living quarters with more energy and resoluteness than before. "I hardly ever go out unless Chip's with me."

"Steady date, eh?" Gar asked the question in a dubious tone.

Ann colored slightly. "Sort of."

"You know what Chip told me, one night over at the hospital?" Mrs. Julian's pride apparently extended itself to the handsome young leader of the Colton Conquests. "He said he thought what Annie's doing takes more – he used the word 'guts' – more guts than anything any of the other kids around here do. That's fine, isn't it? For him to start seeing that?"

Later, over dinner at a candle-lighted Italian restaurant downtown, Gar and Donna discussed the new sphere of influence Ann Julian had opened. Because the newly blossomed love they shared was too precious

139

to jeopardize with arguments, they discussed the situation carefully. Gar conceded that Donna's impulsive project had produced "a great many positive results," and Donna agreed that a carefully thought-out overall plan might have circumvented aggression on Tabby Lacer's part.

"That would be a terrific step forward, though, wouldn't it?" Donna asked. "To get Chip O'Neill pulling on our side?"

Gar, as usual, was less optimistic. "Not if he's too rushed. It could backfire. Look, he falls in love with a girl who's decided to walk the straight and narrow. He's already expressed admiration for what she's doing; it takes more guts to break away from a girl gang than to run one. There's more prestige to being a Candy Striper than just another purse-snatcher in tight black pants. Great. By Chip's standards, the ultimate condition is not to be chicken, and Ann's proven that she isn't. Just walking to and from school takes what the kids call hair. So, he finds Ann appealing."

"It couldn't be because she's been looking prettier than all the Tabby Cats put together? She looks like a girl, not a freak."

"That's part of it. An immense part of it. What I'm thinking of is . . . here's the leader of a rough, tough, cop-hating, society-defying

gang. He's suddenly swept off his feet by a –"
Gar shot Donna an amused glance. "By a cute
bundle of fresh enthusiasm, bent on reform.
Any similarity between that description of
Ann and a certain pediatrics nurse is purely
intentional. Okay; to keep *this* girl, he's got
to fly right. Where does that place him in the
eyes of his gang?"

"If they really look up to him," Donna
suggested, "he might start a new trend."

"I wish you were right. Trouble is, you
don't know Chip's buddies. And you've got
an exalted idea of this boy's past. He didn't get
to be leader of the Colton Conquests because
of his boyish smile, believe me. He had to
be cunning, contemptuous of everything we
consider decent, and he had to be ruthless.
Chains, knives, broken bottles . . . the whole
bit, Donna."

"He's young," Donna said. "He's capable
of changing."

"Yes, *several* times," Gar said pointedly.
"Once, while he's enamored of a rather
adorable rebel in the ranks. Once again
when his followers start a general mutiny
because their captain's gone soft. A gradual
change . . . yes, he could be a tremendously
good influence. But visualize him trying to
stay on top and being a model teen-ager. And
ask yourself if he's going to have the . . . guts

to step off his throne."

"He might," Donna ventured. "There's probably someone dying to take his place."

Gar shook his head. "It doesn't work that way. It's not like resigning as president of a college fraternity. In the jungle, the mighty get eaten alive once they take a step backward."

"His own friends wouldn't . . ."

"Ann's 'old friends' did," Gar reminded her. "I don't like it, Donna. We're already having to keep an eye on Ann . . . and on you, for that matter. The police are hardly in a position to assign a personal escort for Chip O'Neill."

Gar wasn't blaming Donna for the situation that existed; now he was merely stating facts. He was worried. He indicated that the juvenile authorities looked for trouble whenever there was a major shake-up in gang structure. Donna listened, torn between pride for the revolution she had triggered and a fear of the consequences.

They dropped the subject after dinner, enjoying an outdoor movie together, revelling in good conversation and the balmy night as they rode on the river drive in the open convertible, returning to Donna's apartment for coffee and the now inevitable kisses. Gar said nothing more about the Colton

142

Street district gangs and their future. Disappointingly, he made no mention of his own future, either. Or Donna's.

FOURTEEN

On a Thursday evening, two weeks after Ann Julian's release from the hospital, Donna found herself alone in her apartment. Gar had family counseling appointments at the clinic lasting until nine-thirty; he would phone after the last patient left his office, he had promised. If Donna wasn't too tired, he'd stop by on his way home.

Downtown stores were open on Thursday nights; with their marriage date just ten days away, Pam and Dr. Janis had gone off on another of their delirious shopping trips. They had taken to accumulating the materials for domestic bliss with a fervor that made Donna ask if the closed season on buying pots, pans, and table linens were imminent. Every corner of the apartment was crammed with crates and boxes containing household items in which, ironically, the ex-sophisticate and the ex-dedicated bachelor girl seemed to take an almost childish delight. Having traveled lonely courses for a long while, neither Pam nor Walter had built up that circle of friends that makes shopping trips unnecessary. There were no showers scheduled; Donna gave up the idea of honoring her friend with a wedding shower when she tried to draw up a guest list and drew a blank instead. Few gifts could be expected after the simple wedding ceremony that was planned. The future Dr. and Mrs. Janis wasted no regrets on that dismal prospect; chinaware clerks and furniture salesmen probably lighted up when they stepped into a shop.

Donna found herself alone this evening, but not lonely. On the assumption that Gar would drop in later, she devoted most of the time after dinner to rearranging her hair and experimenting with a new supply of cosmetics. (Pam had made an astute appraisal of the latter: "You can tell where a girl stands with a man by her shopping sprees. A few weeks ago I was cornering the market in colognes, like you. I'm at the kitchen-gadget stage now. Watch ... you'll be stocking potato peelers like mad in a little while.")

Satisfied that the new beige lounging ensemble was best enhanced by a lipstick shade called Glowing Persimmon, Donna decided to leave well enough alone. Remembering Gar's remarks about the bizarre makeup flashed by some of the Tabby Cats, she returned to her mirror once more, to tone down eyeshadow that had appeared only faintly exotic when she had applied it a few moments before. There was nothing to do now but wait for the phone to ring. Impossible to read, watch TV, or tackle some minor chore. Gar, and the fact that she would see him again soon, permeated her thoughts. Donna made herself comfortable near the phone table, careful not to wrinkle the silky "at home" costume. (Glamorous, but not *obviously* so; casual, but not *too* casual.)

Her phone rang a few minutes before nine-thirty. Instead of the deep, resonant voice that never failed to thrill her, Donna's "Hello" was followed by a soft, breathy question: "H'lo, *Donna?*"

It was Ann Julian.

"Donna . . . I have to talk to you. Could I come over?"

"Can't you tell me on the phone?"

"I'd rather not. I'm in that booth downstairs at our place . . . it's just about like being out on the sidewalk. *You* know."

"I gather you don't want anyone to hear what you have to tell me."

"Uh-huh. Are you real busy? It's important, honest."

"You shouldn't be out at night, Ann. Is

Chip with you?"

"No, it's *about* him!" There was a desperate ring to Ann's tone.

"Can't wait until tomorrow afternoon, hm?"

"No. *Please!*" Ann paused, then suggested, "I could walk over to the corner and get the bus, or something."

"I'd offer to come there, but I'm expecting Dr. Breverman, Ann."

"Oh. Then . . . you can't talk to me at all tonight? I mean . . . it'd be all right . . . if *he* was there. Actually, I wish he'd be there when I tell you . . ."

There was an abrupt silence. "*Ann?* Ann, are you there?" Donna had a fleeting recollection of the exposed telephone next to the front door of the tenement house. On warm nights, the door was left open. Anyone passing by might . . .

"It's okay. I'm still here."

Donna released her breath. "What was wrong?"

She could barely hear Ann's whisper. "Somebody walked part way up the steps. It's okay, I think. I can't see who . . ."

"You're afraid to talk, aren't you?" Donna guessed.

"Sort of."

"All right, go back upstairs. Stay there . . .

146

Whatever you do, don't get any crazy ideas about walking over to the bus stop."

"But if I don't see you . . ."

"I'm going to phone Dr. Breverman and ask him to pick you up. He's at his office, just a few blocks away."

"What if he doesn't come? How will I know?"

"Stay home. I'll get in touch with you somehow if he can't come for you."

"Okay. Thanks a lot."

"You remember what I said, Ann! Go straight upstairs. Is your mom home?"

"Uh-huh. Tim's asleep."

"All right, stay with them. It shouldn't be more than half an hour."

Donna cut the conversation short and dialed Gar's office number, reaching him immediately.

"Gar, I hope I'm not interrupting."

"No, no. My last appointment left a few minutes ago."

"I was afraid you'd leave the office."

"Without calling you? I just tried. Your line was busy. Tell me his name; I'll throttle the buzzard."

Donna explained the reason for her call, adding, "I know you don't like this, darling. I don't want to get involved after promising you I wouldn't."

147

"You say she sounded frightened?"

"Well . . . worried. And concerned about being overheard."

"Then, for Pete's sake, girl, don't apologize. I can put in a call for police protection if . . ."

"No, she just wants to come here. To tell us something. *Us.* She wanted you to hear it, too."

"I'll see you in fifteen-twenty minutes. Is Ann expecting me?"

"I told her to wait upstairs."

"That's my practical, sensible girl."

Gar, with a wide-eyed, apologetic Ann Julian in tow, appeared at the door shortly afterward. He was too anxious to get the cloak-and-dagger meeting under way to notice Donna's new lounge suit. "Ann hasn't said boo to me all the way here," he said, making himself comfortable on the sofa.

"Sit down, Ann. Relax." Donna motioned to a chair.

Ann occupied the edge of the seat as though she might be forced to flee the room on short notice. "I wanted you to hear this, too, Donna." Without being coaxed, she came directly to the point. "Chip walked me home from the hospital. I'm back on duty, Thursday nights till eight. He met me

148

outside, by the main entrance."

Donna settled down beside Gar. "And?"

"He was all shook. He tried to act like he wasn't, but I could tell there was something bugging him. Well, he finally told me ... you know the way Tabby's been kind of laying low?"

"I haven't seen her around," Donna commented. "Have you, Gar?"

"Not in the past week."

"She's been busy," Ann went on. "Spreading all kinds of lies and stirring up this big rumble. She called Chip up at work. . . . He has this new job in a gas station on Fourteenth and Garvey. . . ."

Gar's brows lifted perceptively. "A *job?*"

"It don't ... it *doesn't* pay too much, but he's pretty good at it, so maybe he'll get a raise. For the summer ... I mean, he can't work full time after September because he's going back to school."

Donna stole a glance in Gar's direction. He was visibly impressed.

"That's not what I wanted to tell you," Ann complained. "The thing is, Tabby called Chip and gave him a whole earful about how his own guys are calling him chicken and how the Marauders . . ."

"Gang from Harding Street," Gar explained to Donna.

149

"The Marauders are making passes at the Tabby Cats. See the Cats don't go around with guys from any other club, just the Conquests, and it's like a . . . sort of an insult . . ."

"A challenge?" Gar asked.

"Yeah. A *challenge*, when a Marauder asks one of the Conquests' chicks – girlfriends – for a date, or makes up to her. Sort of an *honor* thing."

Gar released a weary breath, mangling the language in imitation of the local hoodlums: "And if there's one thing the Conquests is, it's, like, *honorable*."

"Anyway, there's all this stuff going on between the Conquests and the Marauders, and Tabby wants to know if Chip's too scared to do anything about it, or what. And he's almost sure she stirred it all up, just to get him back."

Ann didn't have to explain the peculiar tactics of a jilted gang girl. To Tabby Lacer, getting Chip back meant plunging him into the kind of action in which she could be of service to him.

"It's like Tabby rigged the whole thing," Ann said. "But just the same, it's all true. . . . They've got a rumble set for tomorrow night. If Chip doesn't organize his guys and go in front of them, he'll . . . well, the way the

150

Conquest guys feel about him ... he won't *ever* be able to walk around the neighborhood again."

"Do you know what he plans to do?" Gar asked.

"Tomorrow night?"

"Yes. Did he tell you that?"

Ann studied the carpeting at her feet for a few moments. "He didn't know himself." She turned a pleading look from Gar to Donna and back to Gar again. "He used to think he was a big wheel when he got into fights. Tabby made him feel like he was the greatest. Now, he ... doesn't care what *she* thinks. He's doing okay at the station. ... The boss is going to let him have this old car for two hundred dollars – take only a few bucks out of his pay every week – and Chip said he could fix it up so it runs real cool. And like I told him, nobody could take that car away from him. No cop, nobody. It'd really be *his*."

Ann's eyes had filled with tears while she described that adolescent symbol of success; it was as if Chip were being forced to choose between a car of his own and honor. The situation would have had comic overtones except for the fact that the battles for "honor" were fought with vicious weapons.

"He doesn't want to get into trouble. He doesn't even want to take tomorrow night off.

He's supposed to work."

Donna had a mental picture of Chip O'Neill telling "his guys" that he was unavailable for a rumble . . . because he didn't want to lose his job!

"You're sure you don't know what he plans to do?" Gar demanded.

"No. Honest, Dr. Breverman, I don't know. The thing that scares me is – if he goes, he could get into trouble. Get sent up or . . . hurt. If he doesn't go, the Conquests will get him. They'll bust up the station where he works. . . . They'll gang up on him and maybe kill him."

Gar made a low-keyed whistling sound. "Not to mention the hell that's going to break loose when everybody concerned finds out the police have been tipped off."

Ann's eyes widened with shock. "You mean, they'll figure Chip rat-finked, just to get out of it."

"I mean exactly that," Gar said flatly. He got to his feet, pacing the room, occasionally slapping an open palm with his fist. "It'll be Chip or . . . you, Ann."

"But . . . I didn't *really* fink out, I mean . . . I asked my mom, and she said the best thing would be to tell Donna."

"Little Miss Fix-it," Gar said. "Okay, honey. Suggestions?"

152

"We'll have to let the police know, won't we?" Donna asked.

"That's what you had in mind, wasn't it?" Gar leveled his penetrating stare at Ann.

"Well . . . no."

"You told Donna it couldn't wait until tomorrow. You had to talk to her . . . to us . . . right away. You wanted the rumble *stopped*, didn't you?"

Why was Gar using that biting tone, acting like a prosecuting attorney with a murder suspect on the stand? "Gar . . . honey, she's upset enough!"

It shocked Donna to have her precaution ignored. "What were you going to do, Ann? Tell us there's going to be a rumble and then let us *guess* where it's going to be? Or tell us you don't know, the way you 'didn't know' who beat you black and blue?"

"*No!*"

Donna leaped up, going to Ann's side and placing a protective hand on the girl's shoulder. "Honestly, Gar, if this is a psychological approach . . ."

"You can ask for protection without giving cooperation," Gar persisted. "If you want help you've got to tell us the whole story, Ann. *Where?*"

Ann bit her lower lip, her eyes reflecting her misery.

"Why waste our time? We can't do anything for Chip if you don't tell us where . . . what time?"

Ann looked up at Donna. "I don't . . ."

Gar's intentions suddenly made themselves clear to Donna. "Tell him, Ann!"

"Over by the viaduct," Ann whispered. "Across from the park. Ten o'clock."

"Tomorrow night?" Gar demanded. "You're sure?"

Ann nodded. Then she raised her hands to her face and began to cry.

Donna patted her shoulder. "It's all right, Ann. You've done the right thing."

Later, after Gar had driven Ann back to her home, then returned to Donna's apartment for a discussion of the new developments, Donna let him know that he had done the right thing, too. "She was so confused. Wanting to stop that battle and still ingrained with that code the kids live by."

"The 'no rat-fink' code," Gar said. "Yes. It's not a bad quality, actually. Too bad they apply those high ideals to rotten practices."

"I was furious with you, at first . . . yelling at her that way. Then I realized you wouldn't have gotten the information from her any other way. I know. I tried pleading with her when she was in the hospital. Reasoning with her. And I'll swear she knew right along who

154

beat her up. But the more I tried to get her to name names, the more she refused to talk about it. If you hadn't gotten her to tell you everything tonight, do you know what? She'd have gone home twice as miserable as when she came."

"That's why I yelled. I wanted to shock her into telling."

"I know that now," Donna said. "She can tell herself you forced the information from her. She'll be able to live with her conscience, but . . . maybe you can get the police to solve Chip's problem for him. And that's what Ann really wanted."

Not that breaking up the scheduled rumble would solve any problems permanently, Gar explained. Calling in the authorities would only put a temporary stopper on the poison Tabby had managed to brew up; unless the hostilities were mediated, sooner or later the violence would erupt. "At least it can be delayed," Gar added. "There'll be social workers and probation officers at work, trying to settle the thing – give the kids a chance to cool off. Once it erupts, there's no way to melt it except with more violence, and that only widens the rift between the gangs and the people who are out to help them."

Gar finished the cool drink Donna had poured for him and set the glass on an end

155

table. His brow furrowed, he walked slowly to the broad window overlooking Colton Park. From where he stood, Donna knew, Gar could see the block-long concrete area bordering the Park Street Viaduct. "It's like a stage setting," he said. "All it needs is for the actors to show up." He devoted the rest of his visit to making certain that they didn't – using Donna's telephone to notify the proper authorities, as well as the East Colton Street District residents who might, hopefully, have some influence on juvenile gang members on both sides.

It was nearly midnight when Gar said good night, adding, "I didn't get to tell you how lovely you look tonight."

Donna brushed aside the compliment as though she hadn't devoted several hours to achieving the effect. "Same old me. Nothing special."

"Then you aren't psychic, after all," Gar said lightly. "I thought you might have gotten dressed up for a special occasion I had in mind."

"Like what?"

He kissed Donna's cheek. "We're both too keyed up about this gang fight mess. Besides, it's late. I don't like to rush special occasions. Rain check?"

Bewildered, Donna said, "Sure."

And then spent the better part of a sleepless night wondering what Gar had had in mind.

FIFTEEN

Friday night. A stranger walking into Donna's apartment would not have known that twenty-four hours had passed.

Gar Breverman had again stationed himself at the window, peering anxiously toward the appointed battlefield of the Marauders and the Conquests. In the suspenseful atmosphere that surrounded her, Donna almost forgot about the deferred "special occasion"; she watched, too. And like Gar, she hoped that there would be nothing to see.

But though the scene appeared unchanged, the time that had elapsed between Thursday and Friday nights had been crammed with activity. Since the object of the juvenile officers had been to prevent the fracas rather than to make pointless, wholesale arrests, the word had been spread; the secret rendezvous of the two rival gangs was no longer secret. By cruising the area, the police expected to outwit any attempts to shift the rumble to another location.

157

"I don't know why I'm looking out here," Gar said finally. He turned his back on the window, and Donna walked with him to the dinette table, where she had poured two cups of coffee. "Both gangs know that they'll be greeted by squad cars if they come anywhere near the park. The police hauled Frankie Cedars in for questioning on a theft charge. Hubcaps."

"Who's Frankie Cedars?"

"The Head Marauder. It's just a routine questioning, but that should keep one of the leaders occupied for a few hours. Impossible to round them all up, of course. Or to keep tabs on every hood in the neighborhood. They'll break up anything that even begins to look like a gathering, though. Frankly, I don't expect anything to happen tonight."

"Couldn't it happen tomorrow night?" Donna suggested. "There aren't enough policemen to patrol every alley every minute, day and night."

"True. If the gangs are determined to fight it out, it's inevitable that they will. But, you know, working with these kids we've discovered that most of them don't *want* the bloodshed. It's a herd instinct that drives them, a fear of being left out. Individually, they're insecure. Scared stiff. In a mob, they can hide their fear." Gar smiled a rueful smile. "It's a kind of togetherness – with baseball bats and steel knuckle rings."

Donna made a shuddering motion. She watched Gar sip his coffee and glance at his watch. "What time do you have?"

"Ten fourteen."

"And all's quiet on the Park Street front. I just hope Ann's staying home, where she belongs. If Tabby really engineered the fracas, she must be furious by now. She'll be looking for . . . someone she can blame."

"Ann's going to be sensible."

"And Chip?"

"I told you what the desk sergeant said when I called the station awhile ago. Chip's at work. A squad car's checking on him at regular intervals." Gar twisted his face into one of his wry, disbelieving expressions. *"That* I'd like to see! The incorrigible O'Neill kid wiping windshields. And trusted with a gas station cashbox!"

"He's in love," Donna pointed out.

"You believe in the miracle cure?" Gar set his coffee cup into the saucer and rose to his feet. Circling the table, he bent over to cup Donna's face in his hands. "Or just in the miracle, period?"

"I believe . . ." Donna said. The deep blue eyes probed hers. "In the miracle . . . period."

"I want this for keeps, Donna. I hope you

159

do, too." Gar didn't wait for a reply; he must have read it in Donna's eyes. "I'm asking you to marry me, darling. Am I doing badly?"

"You're doing beautifully, Gar."

"For an amateur. It's my first and only proposal. I've never known anyone else I wanted to have next to me for the rest of my life."

Donna moved upward, sliding easily and naturally into his arms. "Gar . . . oh, Gar, don't tell me this isn't a miracle. Someone so perfect for me . . . wanting me."

"Soon, Donna?"

"I hope so. Oh, I hope so!"

There was no obstacle to their love. No decision to make now except to define "soon." They moved to the living room, too engrossed in planning their life together even to think of looking down into the streets below.

It was shortly after eleven when the shrill cry of the telephone intruded into their quiet conversation.

Gar frowned. "Who could that be?"

Donna started across the room. "I can't imagine. If you hadn't just called the police station, I'd think it was trouble."

Donna lifted the receiver as the phone rang again. "Hello?"

"Donna, I'm scared!" Ann's shrill cry

escaped the receiver, bringing Gar to his feet.

"What's wrong? Ann, what are you doing up at this . . ."

"I haven't seen Chip. He never got here."

Annoyed with what seemed to be senseless hysteria, Donna said, "He's not supposed to be at your place. He's gone home. Dr. Breverman talked to a friend in the police department just a few minutes ago. Everything's quiet. Chip left the gas station at eleven o'clock. Driving. He's probably asleep by now."

"Oh, *no!* No, he's not."

"Ann, there hasn't been any fighting. The police made sure there wasn't anyone hanging around the gas station or around Chip's house."

"Well, he's not home," Ann cried. "He's supposed to be here, like he said."

Donna turned to Gar, who was standing beside her now. "Can you hear this?"

Gar nodded, his expression grave.

"Ann? What made you think Chip was supposed to come to your place? After *eleven o'clock?*"

Ann was in tears by now. "I called him at the gas station. Just before he went off the job. See . . . I didn't know what was going on. I couldn't stand it, just staying home and no way of knowing what was . . ."

"Did he *tell* you he'd come to see you after he left the station?"

"Just for a minute, to show me his car. His boss let him have that car, like he promised. Chip said he'd just drive up and let me see it. He was all jazzed – he never had a car before – so my mom said okay, but I couldn't go for a ride or anything, just *see* it, and after he really fixed it up . . ."

Gar gestured with his head and reached for the telephone.

"Dr. Breverman wants to talk to you, Ann."

Gar took the instrument from Donna. "Ann? Are you positive Chip was going to your place first? Before going home?"

"I dunno." Ann sounded confused. "He sort of said . . ."

"Said *what?*" Gar demanded.

"Well, if the cops were tailing him when he left work, what he'd do was to go home and make like he was going to bed . . . you know, leave the lights on so they could see him. And then after they left, he'd . . . like, sneak out and come over here for a few minutes."

Gar released a disgusted sigh. "Great! This is why the police are knocking themselves out to protect you kids. So that you can play peekaboo behind their backs."

"Gee, I'm sorry, Dr. Breverman. Maybe it

162

wasn't such a cool idea."

"A cool idea it definitely was not," Gar said. "But there's no need for you to get hysterical. If Chip went home first, he's probably playing possum over there, with a squad car under his window. So he's very, very safe. And another thing, young lady. When you get panicky because you and your boyfriend have engineered some kooky deal like this, you call the *police*, not . . ."

Ann filled the receiver with tearful apologies once more. Then she said, "All I can ever think of . . . I mean, I'm so used to calling Donna . . ."

"Blessed Donna," Gar muttered. "Patron saint of idiotic teen-agers! I told you we just talked to the police department. Everything's under control, so I'd assume your boyfriend . . ."

"I saw him go by," Ann said abruptly.

"You *what?*"

"That's why I got scared and called. I saw him drive by. He told me to watch for this dark green '50 Buick he's got. He drove by once, real slow, like he was looking for somebody, and then this other car's been cruisin' around the place."

"Probably looking for a parking space," Gar said. "That street's always crowded at the curb. It certainly doesn't sound like Chip's being chased by anyone."

"Oh no. No." There was a silence, as though Ann might be wondering why she had made the call in the first place.

"Look, Ann. Go on upstairs and stay there."

"But I promised Chip . . ."

"Upstairs," Gar ordered. "And stay there! We've had enough trouble without you kids going out of your way to look for it. Understand what we want you to do?"

Ann's reply was too indistinct for Donna to hear it; she assumed it was a chastened, "Yessir."

Gar banged the receiver into place."Jellybrained kids! The whole area in an uproar, tension so thick you can't cut it with a cleaver, and what's on their minds? Eluding police protection, so that they can drool over a jalopy!" He was walking the length of the living room as he spoke, fuming with anger.

"I honestly thought Ann had more sense," Donna said. "Or that her mother would have put her foot down. If Ann's been checking the traffic, she's probably been out on the steps. In that neighborhood, at this hour!"

"In my field, you stop being surprised by the crazy things people do." Gar looked deep in thought, half muttering the rest to himself.

164

"Maybe Chip didn't see the girl and decided to go for a ride alone. Or maybe he saw the police trailing him . . . decided to go home and hit the sack for real." Gar crossed the room once more, apparently more disturbed than angry now. "I hate to keep bugging the police every time Ann gets some wild idea into her head. They can only spread themselves so thin . . . probably watching the characters who *wanted* trouble tonight." He started for the door. "I'll be back, honey."

"Where are you going?"

"I thought I'd drive past Ann's place. If I see Chip, I'll give him a piece of my mind and see that he goes home."

Donna moved forward. "I'll go with you."

"It's not necessary . . ."

"I'd be too nervous staying here." Donna hesitated. "Should we let the police know?"

"They're probably swarming all over the neighborhood." Gar shrugged his shoulders. "I know I'm contradicting myself. All I want to do is drive past Ann's and make sure those two numbskulls don't get together for a midnight auto show." Gar had opened the door, making no objection when Donna stepped out into the hall in front of him. He grinned nervously. "Maybe they'll decide to test the front seat . . . see if it's comfortable for making out."

165

"Spoilsport."

"They break up my evening, I'll break up theirs," Gar said. He meant it facetiously, but his tone had a serious ring to it. And Donna noticed that he was walking so rapidly that she could barely keep step with him.

There was never a time when the East Colton Street district was completely devoid of traffic. As Gar cruised the neighborhood, Donna peered at cars that passed them occasionally, or craned her neck hopefully when old-fashioned headlights indicated that an oncoming car might be the dark green model driven by Chip O'Neill.

"He wasn't parked along the curb in Ann's block," Donna repeated for perhaps the third time. "I'm sure he's gone home by now."

"We drove by his place not five minutes ago," Gar reminded her. There had been no Buick parked within a three-block radius of Chip's home; the dilapidated three-story tenement building had been dark. "For all we know, we're chasing wild geese. For all we know, he didn't take the car out of the gas station tonight. Maybe he couldn't get it started. Who knows?"

Donna yawned. "We should have reported Ann's message to the police."

Gar nodded, turning once more into a

166

street that would take them past Ann's doorway. "We'll have one more look and forget the whole thing." Under his breath he mumbled something about silly people wearing themselves out playing wet nurses to kids who should be able to take care of themselves. Then, catching the reflection of headlights in his rearview mirror, he asked, "That's an older car behind us, isn't it?"

Donna had caught a glimpse of the car moments before as it turned from Gaffers Street into their own lane. "It's not a '50 Buick. Anyway, Chip wasn't driving. Looked like a carload of people, from what I could see."

They crossed a narrow dead-end alley that bisected two sections of a huge auto-parts warehouse. Donna's eyes searched the darkness. As they passed the alley, Donna said, "I could be wrong, but that could have been . . ."

Gar had already slowed down. "I think I saw it, too. Two-tone job. Some dark color with gray on top."

"Can you back up?"

"Wait a minute." Gar was looking into his rearview mirror. "That car behind us . . ."

"They're turning off," Donna said. She had spun around in her seat, seeing the twin beams that had been following them swing around into the alley.

"Nobody'd have any legitimate business there at this hour. Nothing there, as I recall it, except a couple of loading platforms." By the dim light of the dashboard, Donna saw Gar frown. "I'm wondering if we shouldn't report it. Or go back and have a look?"

Donna felt a quivering under her ribs. "Whatever you do, don't get involved."

Gar had thrown the car into reverse. "Don't worry. I just want a quick look." Their car formed a wall across the alley entrance now. "No getting out of the . . ."

"Breverman! Doc!"

The shrill feminine scream came from the alley, freezing them for a moment.

"Breverman! Help! They're gonna kill him!"

In the next breath, Gar was leaping out of the car, gasping orders: "Get in my seat. Keep the motor running . . . keep it in gear . . . lock the door. If anyone comes near the car, gun it . . . get the cops!" He was racing into the narrow passage, yelling the words as he ran. For a few seconds he was out of her sight, then she saw him, caught by the other car's headlights now illuminating the alley.

"Gar, don't go out there!"

Donna's cry was lost in the bedlam that had erupted in the alley. She edged into the driver's seat without swerving her shocked stare.

It was like a flashing series of horror pictures involving totally unexpected characters. What was Tabby Lacer doing here, screaming at Gar for help? Jo-Jo and Nicki were just barely visible, skulking in the shadows of the warehouse, looking uneasy and as though they might run from the scene at any instant.

Gar must have seen the three hoodlums surrounding the old gray and green Buick before Donna saw them. With Tabby running beside him, filling the alley with shrieks that reverberated from the high surrounding walls, Gar had torn straight toward the trio. They were pummeling a wildly swinging figure with their fists as Gar approached. Chip O'Neill. Surrounded, Chip was flailing his arms in what looked like a grotesque dance.

There was one instant in which all the attention was concentrated on Chip. Then, as Donna watched, breathless, there was a flash of something metallic; a sudden knife in the hands of one of the assailants. Gar dived for the attacker, but he was too late. Once, twice, then again and again Donna saw the blade lifted and plunged into the boy's midsection. If he screamed, the sound was drowned out by a terrified cry from Tabby.

Insane flashing pictures: Tabby swinging a tire iron; the knife-wielding thug crumpling to the cement in almost the same second as his victim.

Actors on a brilliantly lighted screen, with the film run at twice its normal speed! One of the thugs lunged forward, and Donna saw Gar execute what looked like a figure from a Chinese ballet. Only that strangely graceful Oriental motion, and the young hood was flat on his back; the thud of his body slamming against the concrete was audible even inside the closed car.

Tabby was grappling with the third member of the gang, yelling for Jo-Jo and Nicki to hit him with the tire iron he had wrenched from her hand.

The girls moved forward too slowly and reluctantly to pose any threat. Gar flung himself around to come to Tabby's rescue. The young punk must have decided that fighting was only fun when the odds were on his side. He kicked at Tabby, his foot connecting with her shin. She stumbled, and the hood gave her a massive shove with one arm, pushing her against Gar, throwing them both off balance. Before Gar could recover his equilibrium, the third member of the gang was racing out of the alley, leaving the car and his fallen companions behind

170

him. Blood-smeared, obviously terrified, he hesitated for a moment as he saw Donna. She felt her stomach flip over as he moved toward the car door. Perhaps the racing motor frightened him off. Or maybe he had noticed that the locking button was pushed down. More likely he realized that Gar would catch up to him before he could force himself into the car for a quick getaway. He paused only for a split second; then he was charging down the street as though someone had set his long, ducktailed hair on fire.

Tabby's anguished cries snapped Donna out of her shock. Ignoring Gar's instructions, she got out of the car, her legs shaking as she entered the alley. Piercing light from the abandoned automobile illuminated a bloody battlefield. No one was paying any attention to the young member Gar had flattened; he lay on his back, twitching occasionally and groaning. His buddy lay only a foot from Chip O'Neill, his head resting in a widening pool of blood.

Gar, Tabby and her less heroic Cats had formed a semicircle around Chip. It wouldn't have required a nurse experienced in Emergency Service to realize that he was critically wounded. All color had been drained from his battered face. He had wrapped his arms around his body in an instinctive but futile effort to stay the well of blood bubbling from the multiple stab wounds below his ribs; his white mechanic's overalls were soaked with it.

Gar was kneeling beside Chip, trying to ignore Tabby's hysteria. He looked up as Donna approached. "It doesn't look like you can do anything for him."

Donna had already verified that fact in her mind. "We need an ambulance from County. One of you girls . . . there's a public phone in the building where Ann lives. The door downstairs is always unlocked. Hurry!"

She was bending over Chip's unconscious form, seeing the hopelessness of any first aid attempt. Chip moaned, and Tabby bent down, reaching out to lift his head. "Don't touch him!" Donna ordered. "Don't touch *any* of them!"

For answer, Tabby drew herself upright. Making a choking animal sound, she aimed a vicious kick into the side of the boy who had used the knife. He let out a loud, "Aa-argh!"; his body jerked violently, and then he was still. "That's how I'll touch *him!*" Tabby cried.

Gar's face had turned livid. "You . . . swine!"

Tabby had been injured herself, but she found energy enough, before Gar or Donna

172

could stop her, to repeat the murderous act. "He killed Chip! He got me to frame him! The dirty, rotten rat . . ." This time the kick was more severe. And this time there was no reaction from the victim.

"Stop that, you maniac! Get ambulances!" Donna yelled. None of the girls moved. "All right, *I'll* go make the call. Gar, see that they don't move Chip." She got to her feet, glaring at Tabby. "I wouldn't kick that kid again, if I were you. You might have cracked his skull in self-defense. Murder is something else again!"

Tabby had stopped shrieking. At Donna's sharp command, her mouth twisted into an ugly snarl. Under the glaring headlights, the luminous white lipstick, the smudges of blood, and the heavily penciled eyes – eyes glinting with merciless hatred – made her look more than ever like something painted on a cheap carnival poster advertising a Spook House. In a thick, gutteral voice, she said, "I kicked a lotta guys' ribs in fer less."

Surprisingly, her reptilian redheaded friend, Nicki, backed the statement up. "I seen her do it. Don't forget Chilidog knifed 'er boyfriend."

As though that justified everything! "Her boyfriend's going to bleed to death. *Get going!*"

Tabby moved forward. "No call. We get

173

Chip in your car. Take care of him at *your* place." She indicated Donna with a thrust of her chin.

"You're insane!" Donna cried. "He doesn't have much chance as it is, but he's still alive. If he gets emergency surgery he might . . ."

Donna's plea for reason was wasted on Tabby. Her hysteria reduced, she had suddenly taken command. "*You* . . . Doc! Get holda Chip's arms. We'll get his feet."

"You can't move him out that way! You'll kill him!" Donna started toward the end of the alley. "I'll get the ambulances. They'll be here in a . . ."

Tabby's order was barely audible. It was more a toneless grunt. "Nick . . . *keep 'er here.*"

The redhead hesitated for only one second. Then she bent over swiftly, coming up with a gory object in her hand. It was the switch-blade knife that had been used on Chip.

"What do you think you're doing?" Gar demanded. "You're wasting precious time! Let . . ."

While he spoke there was a swift, catlike motion. In almost the same instant, Donna felt the sharp point of steel pressing against her back.

"Okay, keep actin' smart, there's gonna be more blood," Tabby said. "Keep that carver

174

on 'er, Nicki. So when I tell this creep to get Chip inna car, he'll *move*."

Gar had gone pale. Incredulous, he asked, "If you don't kill him moving him . . . what do you hope to accomplish in Donna's apartment? Who's going to help the kid *there?*"

"You fix him up."

"You must be . . ."

"You're a doctor, aren't you? She's a nurse. Okay. So do somethin' right now. Stop all that bleedin'."

"I'm not a medical doctor," Gar protested. "I'm a psychologist."

"A doctor's a doctor," Tabby snarled. "They wouldn' let you call y'self a doctor, you wasn't one. So quit stallin' me. Get him over where you c'n work on 'im."

"Tabby . . ."

Donna's plea was cut short. "You heard me! If Chip don't make it, I'm gonna let Nicki use the botha yez fer target practice."

Donna risked one more appeal. "Tabby, please listen to me. Even if we were qualified to perform surgery, we couldn't do it without instruments, without anesthetics and . . ." The madness of Tabby's demand couldn't be expressed in words. "*Listen,* Tabby! Chip's probably bleeding internally. He'll have to be opened up . . . the perforation has to be sewn . . ."

Tabby's face, always chalky, looked completely bleached now. Some of the cocky assurance faded from her voice. "You can do *somethin'*. You gotta do somethin'! You better not let nothin' happen t' Chip!"

"I'm not a surgical nurse. Dr. Breverman isn't even licensed to give out pills. Every second that goes by . . ."

"I don't want no cops! I promised Chip I wouldn't get him mixed up with no fuzz!"

"*You* can get out of here if you want to. We'll get him to the hospital." The senselessness of Tabby's demands infuriated Donna. "Look, if he dies here because you didn't let us get help for him, you'll be responsible. You're letting him die because you're too stupid to . . ."

"Shut up!" Donna's head snapped back as Tabby's palm slammed across her cheek; she felt the cracking sound reverberate inside her brain.

Gar's angry leap forward was stopped by Nicki's menacing move. Donna felt the tip of the knife blade move from her back to the base of her neck. She blinked hard, shaking her head as Gar's eyes caught hers for a brief moment. Through the blur, she saw him lift his face, jutting out his chin. It was a subtle, wordless message: *Tabby's frightened. Chip's the one soft spot in her armor. You stay strong.*

176

Hit her where she's weak!

Donna tossed her head back defiantly, ignoring the smarting pain of her cheek. "That'll get you far, Tabby! That'll save Chip's life."

Tabby's attempt to command was strident now, showing open terror. "*Do* something for him!"

"*You* do it," Donna said. "I can't. There's nothing I can do, and I'll witness this much in a courtroom. The three of you deliberately kept us from getting help that might have saved Chip's life!"

Jo-Jo looked toward Nicki, her glance uneasy. Gar seized the cue. "You two haven't done time yet. You'll be starting out at the top, with a nice long stretch for manslaughter." He paused for effect. "Or *murder.*"

"He's lyin'," Tabby cried. "He's a doctor. We'll tell the cops he wouldn't help . . ."

"There's your brainy leader!" Donna addressed the other two girls. "Why won't she let us get Chip to the hospital? Why doesn't she run, if she's afraid of the police? They'll be here soon. We phoned them just before we came here. She's either too stupid or too rattled to think straight."

"Shut up! Do somethin'!" Tabby shrilled. Her eyes darted from Donna to Nicki, then to

Jo-Jo. She must have sensed their uncertainty. "Don't let her con you. Gimme that knife, Nick ... I'll show 'er who's rattled. I know what I'm doin' ... *I always do!*"

Neither of the girls made any response.

"Get out," Gar advised them. "Are you going to spend the next ten years behind bars because Tabby doesn't know a psychologist from a surgeon?"

"I can't stand that bleedin'!" Tabby's scream came from the depths of fear and frustration. *"Do somethin'!* Do somethin' or I'll stick *you!"* Tabby made a wild move to snatch the knife from Nicki's hand. The redhead moved aside, removing the threat to Donna.

"Don't mess about with me!" Tabby spat out a volley of furious profanity. "Give it here!"

Apparently Tabby's furious shout had reached Chip O'Neill's sleeping consciousness. He stirred, rolling his head from side to side. A sound escaped his lips, and Tabby turned her frantic attention to him.

"Chip! Honey, listen ... I didn't know the guys would pull a knife. I made the date because Chilidog said he wanted ... Chip? *Listen ...*"

There was a rasping noise from Chip; a familiar rattle that chilled Donna. And

178

then, barely audible, a single muttered word. "Ann . . ."

Tabby's face seemed to freeze. And Gar drove the message home: "Ann would know what to do. She'd get him into hospital."

Panic swept over Tabby. "You could do somethin' *now!*" She released another string of curses and threats, her hysteria mounting.

"Ann Julian wouldn't let him die." Gar drove his message home in a firm, accusing tone. "Ann wouldn't let her friends take a manslaughter rap."

"Get back here!"

Nicki and Jo-Jo were bolting toward the street.

"You dirty, filthy rat-fink! Gimme that!" Tabby hurled herself at the slimmer girl, stopping her, grabbing her wrist and twisting it. They were grappling for the knife as Gar seized each of them by the forearm, forcing their heads downward. The knife fell from Nicki's hand, clinking to the cement. Donna bent over to pick it up, shuddering at its slimy touch.

"Got it?" Gar asked.

"Yes."

He let Nicki go, still struggling to keep Tabby from clawing and kicking. Nicki waited for one microinstant, her cold eyes surveying the scene. Then she whirled and

179

ran, passing Jo-Jo just before the plump girl rounded the corner, out of sight.

"They . . . ran out on you," Gar said. His breath came hard. Holding Tabby at bay, he repeated the message. "You're all alone, Tabby. If you'll . . . stop acting like a . . . wildcat, we can try to save Chip."

It was as if someone had punctured a wildly fluttering balloon. Tabby stopped the helpless flailing motions. Her body stiffened and she stumbled forward as Gar relaxed his hold on her arm. Then she dropped to her knees at Chip's side, her shoulders jerking convulsively. If she was crying, she was crying inside; there was no sound, and no tears blotched the clown face, already smeared with blood and mascara.

Gar stood over her, trying to regain his breath. "Don't you want to run with the pack? We're going to call for ambulances. The police will . . ."

"Gar . . . *hurry!*" Donna was already moving toward the end of the alley.

Tabby had closed her claw-nailed fingers over Chip's hand. Like Gar, she was breathless, her words coming out in broken gasps. "*Cold.* How come . . . his hand's . . . *so cold?*" Her expression had a frightening, zombilike quality now. "Why's his hand so *cold?*"

180

She repeated the question over and over, her thin plaintive cry following Gar and Donna as they hurried to call for help.

SIXTEEN

There were six of them in the small consultation room adjoining the administrative offices at County Hospital. Two uniformed police officers conducted the investigation. A young man who was introduced as a psychiatric social worker from the city's welfare department, and who had had occasional contact with some of the Conquests, had asked for and been given permission to sit in. Gar and Donna had finished giving their version of the night's carnage. Now it was Tabby Lacer to whom the questions were being directed.

Her glassy-eyed stare had not changed; she might still have been back in the warehouse alley, begging someone to tell her why Chip's hands were so icy. She replied to direct questions tonelessly, like someone under sodium pentothal, her eyes fixed on some undetermined spot on the opposite wall.

"Yeah, I was mad at Chip. Sure. He

dropped me fer this Ann. He chickened out when the Marauders challenged his gang. Why wouldn' I be burned? All the Conquest guys were sore. Then a couple of 'em started gettin' real salty, sayin' Chip was a rat-fink. Like they were gonna really put him down."

"They told you this?" one of the police officers asked.

"Yeah. So I started gettin' scared. I was mad at Chip, sure. The thing is, I didn't want his own guys to do nothin' to Chip. So I told these two wheels . . . the two biggest Conquest guys after Chip . . ."

"These were the two you call Chilidog and Pipes?" the second officer interrupted.

"Yeah. Them. I told them Chip was playin' it cool, that was all. He didn' fink out, like they thought. He knew somebody let the word out about the rumble, so why should the Conquests show up at the viaduct, when the Marauders were hip an' prob'ly wouldn' come, anyway? Chip was workin' at a square job to take the heat off . . . to confuse the law.

"These guys, they acted like they believed me, but they said they wanted to talk to Chip about when he was settin' up another date. They didn't wanna go see him at the gas station, because the cops kept cruisin' by there. So I called him up at the station.

"At first, Chip said he didn't want to see

nobody. He said he'd get all the guys together an' explain what he wanted to do – not just drop the Conquests all of a sudden, like Julian dropped the Cats. He knew what happened that time . . . that wasn't too cool."

Tabby looked bewildered at this point. She had referred to the brutal attack on Ann Julian as though she had not been responsible for it, and suddenly she seemed to remember otherwise. The result was a long, vacant-staring silence.

"What happened then?" There was a patient gentleness in the policeman's prodding question. No one listening to Tabby could doubt that she was ill.

"Then Chip said he had someplace else to go. He had this car and he wanted to show it to somebody. I asked him was it Julian and he said that was *his* business. So I knew.

"I was mad about that. I was worried about him, though. Sort of mixed up; like, I wanted to get back at him, but I didn't want nothin' bad to happen to him. I dunno. I guess I figured if I was there, I could talk Chilidog an' Pipes into not gettin' rough. I dunno." Tabby ran a shaky hand over her face. "I dunno what I was thinkin'. I got Chip to say he'd meet the guys over by the warehouse. Me an' Jo-Jo an' Nicki, we even went with the guys. All the way there, they acted like they wasn't mad or nothin'. Then when Chilidog jumped outta the car, he hollered now was my chance to get even about Julian. Them guys ... they thought I was puttin' on a act ... that I was gonna help 'em work Chip over!"

Tabby's recollection of what had happened after that was strangely blank. She shuddered, rubbing her eyes with the heel of her hand. "I can't remember. All I wanna know ... is he dead? Chip. Is he dead?" The zombi voice took on an anxious pitch, but Tabby's eyes didn't move from the blank wall.

"He was still in Surgery ten minutes ago," Donna said. She had stepped outside the room during part of the questioning, to ask about Chip at the third-floor charge desk. She got up again now. "If you don't need me, Officer, I'll go back upstairs and check."

"We're about finished here," the policeman told her. He stood up, indicating to the others that the session was over. There was a general scraping of chairs; only Tabby remained seated. Someone knocked at the door, and Gar turned to open it.

Still dressed in wrinkled green surgical garb, with the tight-fitting cap tied over her hair, Pam Hollis was hardly recognizable for a moment. She looked tired, and she addressed

184

no one in particular. "The O'Neill boy is in Recovery. Dr. Innes said you'd want to know that."

"How is he?" Gar asked.

Pam sighed. "Well, I wouldn't have given him a prayer when they wheeled him in."

"Now?" one of the officers prodded.

"You'll have to ask the doctor."

Donna understood from experience the hopelessness of pressing a nurse for a prognosis. Nevertheless, she asked, "Off the record, Pam. How did he look to you?

Pam drew a weary breath. "Well . . . he was on the table almost two hours. Deep, nasty wounds. It's a miracle they didn't hit a vital organ. As it was, we didn't get him a minute too soon. Time we'd clamped off the bleeders and located the perforations in his colon, the anesthetist said he could barely detect a pulse."

Most of the group had moved into the darkened corridor by now. Only Tabby and one of the officers remained in the room, Tabby listening to the conversation with dazed incomprehension.

"He's a strong, husky kid," Pam concluded evasively. Then, with sudden irritation, she said, "You know better than to ask questions like this. I only came down to report that the O'Neill boy's in Recovery, and the others . . ."

185

Somehow, Donna had half forgotten the others.

"What about them?" Gar asked.

"I didn't see the back injury case. I understand the X rays were negative."

"No fractures," Donna explained to Gar and the other two men.

"The other one's gone."

Pam made the statement as though she thought the news had come down earlier. When there was no response except shocked silence, she said, "I thought you knew. We're shorthanded . . . we've been busy. I expect the charge nurse was tied up, trying to reach the boy's family."

The psychiatric social worker looked stunned. "Family?" he muttered. "That was something Chilidog didn't have, among other things."

"We'll have to come upstairs and get a complete report," the officer said. His tone implied that this was a routine matter. It happened often; it was no strange occurrence, either to a surgical nurse on night duty or to a Colton Street Station cop. "That's the fellow with the skull fracture, right?"

"That's not the way they filled in the 'cause of death' upstairs," Pam said. "I was in a different O.R. when he died, so I can't tell you any more than that."

186

"He didn't die of the head injury?" Gar frowned, probably remembering the ugly wound Tabby had inflicted with the tire iron.

"Ruptured spleen, massive internal hemmorhage," Pam said. She pulled the unflattering surgical cap from her head, revealing her pale, flawlessly groomed hair. "Somebody must have worked him over while he was down." Then, in an enormously weary voice not untinged by disgust, she added, "We get them all the time. Literally get the life kicked out of them."

Donna shuddered. Her eyes met Gar's for an uneasy instant.

If they were recalling the viciousness of Tabby's attack, the officer in charge was remembering their recital of it. He turned back to the open doorway, addressing his partner. "That changes the way we'll book her, Fred."

The other policeman, who had stationed himself beside Tabby's chair, nodded. No one elaborated on the differences between "assault with a deadly weapon" and "murder." And if Tabby knew what their grim exchange meant to her future, she gave no sign of it. She appeared too detached to care what was happening to her; even her concern for Chip was vague and without understanding. When Gar walked back into the room, asking

Tabby the simplest of questions – her name, what she was doing here, if she realized what had happened – there was no response at all.

The door was closed, and the group proceeded to the bank of elevators off the hospital's main reception room.

"You folks can go home, if you like," the officer said to Gar. "We'll be in touch with you before the inquest."

"I'd like to get Miss Marker home," Gar said. "I know she's exhausted."

"I couldn't sleep," Donna told him. "Let me go up and find out how Chip's coming along. I'll want to stop at Ann Julian's on the way home. She ought to be told what's happened."

Gar lifted his eyes ceilingward for a brief, critical instant.

"We're going over to talk to Miss Julian," the officer said. "After we get the Lacer girl booked."

"I wanted to ask you about that," Gar said. "Were you planning to take her down to the station? Tabby?"

There was a mildly sarcastic edge to the reply. "Under the circumstances, what would *you* suggest?"

"I'd suggest contacting Dr. Van Veerlin. He's head of the psychiatric staff here. I think she should be admitted for observation, and

188

it'll take an M.D. to do that."

They discussed the legal technicalities for a few moments, and then the officer asked, "You think she's flipped, Doctor? What is it, shock, maybe? I've seen people go into that . . . what is it you people call it . . . a catatonic state?"

Gar nodded.

"I've seen people do that when they suddenly realize they're facing a murder rap."

"She's not even aware that she killed someone. No, it's not simple shock. She's lost her identity . . . she's disintegrated."

The officer checked the light panel above the elevators. "There's one on the way down." He seemed to have no desire to explore the ramifications of Tabby's condition.

"She's gone through life rejecting everything," Gar persisted. "Family, law, order . . . society, as we know it. She constructed a whole new social structure for herself, and a false image of herself and the people around her. Suddenly the structure begins to crumble. One of her gang members quits. Chip O'Neill deserts his gang *and* Tabby in exchange for a square job and a comparatively unglamorous girlfriend. That's the beginning."

The young man from the city welfare department had been following Gar's reasoning with avid interest. "Maybe the final blow came when her friends walked out on her. The two girls you told us about, Doctor."

"Exactly. She stopped being Tabby." Gar turned to the officer. "You wouldn't have gotten a word out of her tonight if her whole identity hadn't been smashed. You've had her in for questioning before, haven't you?"

The policeman released a low, whistling breath. "Don't remind me."

"There you are. If she weren't very, *very* sick, she'd have clammed up. Lived by the code, figured she'd get her revenge without any help from the law. The way she got her revenge in the alley."

An elevator arrived. The doors opened and they stepped into the cage. On the way up to the surgical floor, Donna said, "You've been wanting to break through that tough shell for a long time, Gar. Will it be easier now?"

"She's not in touch with reality. I don't know. Maybe all we'll find if we ever get past that shell now are . . ."

"Fragments," the psychiatric social worker predicted. "Pieces of a personality."

"Just fragments," Gar echoed.

It wasn't what Gar had wanted. Under his own shell, under his often cynical facade,

Donna suspected that his compassion was deeper than her own.

To Gar, there was no deeper tragedy than to see a human being cross that line beyond which the most able psychiatrists and psychologists cannot reach to pull him back. He was too devoted to his profession to make hasty predictions, but he was not above deep personal concern for the Tabbies of the world. And either instinct, experience, or intuition told him that the outlook for Tabby Lacer was not bright.

He said as much, in exactly those words. "But then," he added, "it wasn't too bright the day she was born."

Donna had the distinct impression that he was more depressed about Tabby's condition than she was at the word they received at the third-floor nurses' station: Chip O'Neill's name was still on the "critical" list.

SEVENTEEN

A hard-working surgical team had gotten Chip O'Neill over the first hurdle; Ann Julian was trying, with prayerful determination and a not-too-convincing cheerfulness, to get him

191

over the second. Although Chip had survived the brutal knifing, Donna's bright vision of a happy ending was beginning to fade.

Four days had passed since Chip had been brought to the hospital. Now he lay in his bed, shoulders propped up by a pillow, his uneasy attitude making it clear that he wished Donna and Gar would cut their visit short.

"Don't expect miracles," Gar had warned in the hospital elevator. "Don't expect a movie ending. Chip isn't going to become an eagle scout. We haven't seen the last gang fight around East Colton Street."

Donna had attributed the remark to Gar's ingrained cynicism. Or perhaps his negative attitude was based on disappointments of his own; certainly his best efforts had failed to reach Pipes, the other member of the Conquests gang who had survived the fracas. And Tabby Lacer, confined in the hospital's psychiatric ward, had sunk deeper into her isolation from reality.

But now, with Ann Julian looking pert in her Candy Striper uniform, and making a pathetic attempt to lend a party spirit to the visit, Donna bean to doubt some of the rosy plans she had outlined, mentally, for Chip O'Neill. When there was an optimistic tone to the conversation, it came from Ann, or

192

from Donna herself. Gar was silent most of the time, observing and listening.

Donna searched for additional hopeful ideas. "Well, you'll be back on the job soon, won't you, Chip?"

"What job?" he asked glumly. "You think the guy at the station wants me back? After all that jazz that was in the papers?"

"He might. I'm sure . . ."

Gar shook his head. It was a warning signal; Chip's boss *didn't* want him back.

"Oh, well, you'll find something you like better. As soon as you get home and start feeling a little stronger . . ."

Chip's face twisted into a bitter expression. "My ol' man don't want me around the house. All the guys at the cab company's givin' him a hard time . . . how I was mixed up in a murder. He don't want nothin' t'do with me." He sniffed his contempt. "So it goes both ways. Who needs *him*?"

Embarrassed, Donna grasped at the only straws left to her. "You have Ann. Between the two of you, you'll . . ."

"We'll what?" Chip asked. "You think I'd have a chance, livin' around here, anyway? You think the Conquest guys are gonna give me a welcome home party when I get outta this joint? My pals? My buddies?" Chip stopped to get his breath, his hand going to a painful spot over his incision. "I'll get a party, okay. This time, instead of two guys, there'll maybe be ten. I goofed it up. I shouldn't of crossed 'em." Chip stared into his covers resentfully. "They ain't about to ferget what happened t' Chilidog."

"But he attacked you! He nearly killed you!"

Chip was looking at her now as though she were a cretin. "Look, I 'preciate what you an' the doc, here, done fer me. Don't think I don't. The trouble with people like you . . . you don't know what it's all about. Know what I mean? You ain't *us*. You got the idea it should all be the way *you* got it figured. It ain't like that."

"You and Ann were moving in the right direction," Donna protested. "I was thinking . . . even if you didn't want to break away from your . . . old friends, you might be able to make them see that . . . fighting like a pack of hyenas won't get them anywhere. In a jail cell, maybe. Or a hospital bed. Or a slab at the morgue. If you could turn all that energy into some positive channel . . ."

Chip eyed her suspiciously. "Like?"

"Oh, like a car club. Or an athletic team. You could still compete with the other . . ."

Chip closed his eyes. "Oh, man! You been readin' fairy tales."

194

Donna's confidence began to falter. It was an effort to continue her positive persuasion, especially when Chip was still too weak to be badgered by arguments. "You might . . . want to go somewhere else, Chip. It's a big country. If it's going to be rough for you around here . . ."

"You know somethin'?" Chip's face assumed a cocky, contemptuous pose. "Here's somethin' you big-shot experts can't get through your heads. All your college . . . all the brains you're supposed to have. You don't even know this much. It's rough anyplace you go! Anyplace you go, you gotta fight, else you get pushed aroun'."

Donna glanced over in Gar's direction. He was eyeing her steadily, reminding her that her small triumph with Ann had not been typical. It was a slow process, sometimes an impossible process. And throwing fresh new obstacles in your way were gas station owners who, sensibly, wanted no part of a gang leader, and fathers who wanted nothing more to do with a son who embroiled himself in alley fights that ended in murder.

Chip summed it up. "You try to play it square an' nice, what does it get you? A shiv in the ribs."

There was only one faintly hopeful note. As Gar and Donna were leaving, Chip said, "I

195

guess you people don't mean no harm. You just don't dig the way it is."

Ann saw them out to the corridor. Obviously uncomfortable, she said, "He's still feelin' lousy. When he feels better, it'll all be different."

"Sure," Gar said.

"I had it figured real different, too," Ann went on. "I thought . . . Chip was always real popular with the girls. Not just the Tabby Cats. When he was still in school, lots of girls used to think he was real cute. So I thought, they'll all be coming here to see him, and maybe . . . like, even some of the gang kids, they'll see how neat it is to be a Candy Striper and have people treatin' you like you're *somebody*."

"How's the recruiting program coming along?" Gar asked. "No takers?"

"Nobody's come around." Tears welled up in Ann's eyes. "I guess the kids still in school don't want to get mixed up with Chip anymore. Or their folks won't let them come around. The gang kids . . . Chip's poison to them now. There's *nobody*. Even his dad won't come and see Chip."

"You'll make new friends," Donna assured her. But the assurance was shaky. "Some of the other girls here . . ."

"I'm the only volunteer here from around

East Colton Street. They're nice to me around the hospital, but I don't see any of them outside of that."

Donna made a few more encouraging statements, most of them platitudes that sounded hollow to her own ears and must have been meaningless to Ann. They said goodbye to her at the elevators, watching her round the corner on her way back to Chip's room. She was off duty tonight, making use of the single all-hours visiting card that is usually issued to the patient's closest relative.

On the way to the ground floor, Donna said, "All right, say it. I took her out of her element. Kids can't stand to be alone . . . they've got to belong somewhere. At least, in the gangs, they weren't social outcasts."

"These two can't go back to the gangs," Gar said. "They're going to be bitter. They may even turn on you because of it."

"I'm sorry," Donna said. "I wish I hadn't . . ."

She felt Gar's hand closing over hers, pressing tightly against her fingers. He was silent until they had gotten out of the elevator and crossed the hospital's foyer and parking lot. Once he had helped Donna into his car and circled to sit beside her in the driver's seat, Gar said, "Don't castigate yourself for what happened, honey. You saw what you

197

thought was an opportunity to help someone. Given the same circumstances, you'd do it again, and I wouldn't blame you. You do the human thing, as you understand it. The small, immediate thing. Right?"

Donna nodded.

"What you've got working against you is the whole fabric of a rotten society these kids have fallen heir to. How do you tear down the slums that spawn them? The kind of parents who are either too discouraged, too ignorant, too tired, or too drunk to make them feel wanted? Chip was right. We lucky ones – we 'experts' – only *think* we understand their problems. Actually, we don't have anything but the most superficial answers. Adult answers. Observe the law, live clean, work hard, think straight. A pack of words. They *see* the kind of world they live in. They *feel* it; they get slapped by it every time they turn around. So where do they turn, Donna? To each other. It may be a slimy rock to cling to, but it's the only rock they've got."

"That's what's bothering me, Gar. Chip and Ann . . . it's as though they're floating off in space right now. And you make it all sound so hopeless . . ."

Gar turned to her swiftly. "Do I? No, you're wrong! This is the *time*, Donna. Oh, maybe not tonight . . . the kid's still wrestling

198

with physical problems, and he's gotten quite a kick in the face from his father, his boss, his alleged friends. But he's free. He's got no choice but to start from scratch. If we play our cards right, go slowly, plant the right seeds and back him up . . ."

"Could we do that, Gar? I realized tonight that all my pat, simple solutions were so idealistic that they were silly. But could we . . ."

"We can make those two kids a project, Donna. Using both our methods. We're catching them in limbo, somewhere between two societies. We'll have to go easy . . . a lot easier than you wanted to go tonight. It's got to spring from *them* – or, at least, it's got to seem that it did. The goal's going to be the same, but prepare yourself for setbacks. Don't be crushed if we fail altogether."

Gar reached for the ignition key and then apparently changed his mind. "We'll have more time with each other. Time to plot it out and work on it together."

"Oh, Gar . . . if we only *could* . . ."

Gar's eyes shone with the challenge, but the challenge became secondary. His arms slipped around Donna. "When did you say Walter and Pam will be taking off on their honeymoon?"

"Later this week."

199

"Apartment's going to be empty?"

"Yes."

"Let's start on our own project first," Gar said simply. He kissed her, coming up for air and returning to kiss her again.

"When?"

"City Hall opens at nine tomorrow. Can you take the morning off?"

Donna pulled his face closer to hers. Around them, the lights of the hospital and the East Colton Street district shone as brightly as stars. "Can you?"

"It won't be like shirking my job." Gar held her a little closer. "It's going to be a matter of taking on reinforcements."

For a long while after that, Donna remained still in Gar's arms, drawing from the strength of him and knowing that he, too, was gathering strength for the future they had chosen together. When, at last, he started the motor, Donna looked up to the lights that illuminated the hospital's third floor. There was hope there, she thought. If you were strong enough yourself, lucky enough yourself . . . if you had love and you weren't alone, you could make that faint hope blossom. Not all over East Colton Street. But up there, where the small seed had already been planted.

"We'll be back," she said.

Gar took his right hand from the steering

200

wheel and placed a firm arm around her shoulders. Steering out of the parking lot and toward the street, he repeated her words. "We'll be back."